CODE OF THE WEST

Stories
by Sahar Mustafah

Willow Books
Detroit, Michigan

Code of the West

Editor: Antoinette Gardner
Cover art: Cécile Graat
Author photo: Michelle Strahan

ISBN 978-0-9992232-1-5
LCCN 2017951694

Grand Prize Winner, Willow Books Literature Awards, 2016

Willow Books, a Division of Aquarius Press
www.WillowLit.net

Printed in the United States of America

For Sabah & Sabrine,
banat arrab

and for Khalid,
enta omri

Move leisurely, Life, so that I can see you
with all the loss about me. How much I have forgotten you
in your crossways, seeking me and you.

—Mahmoud Darwish, "Now in Exile"

CONTENTS

Code of the West

Three days after Letti Vega disappeared, her body was found in an excavated lot. Her bottom half was naked and bruised. A construction crew had drained a large hole of rainwater and discovered her face-down. Her feet were steeped to her ankles in the wet clay, and her long brown hair was tangled like reeds around her shoulders.

Two Watford City detectives showed up at the trailer park. They waited for Riyad Nasrrawi at the entrance. They were leaning against a shiny black Tahoe, smoking cigarettes and flicking the ashes away from their shoes.

Riyad shivered as soon as he stepped out of the trailer. The brisk morning air penetrated his sweatshirt. The start of September had been cold and wet.

"Did you have any interactions with Ms. Vega outside the restaurant?" the first detective asked him. His brown hair thinned across the crown. He was pudgy and a few inches shorter than Riyad.

"No," Riyad answered. He wasn't sure what to do with his hands as he stood there for the interrogation. He finally stuck them in the pouch of his sweatshirt and rubbed his key medallion inside the fold with his thumb.

"Do you know anyone who would want to harm her?"

Henry Elbert's face flashed across his mind. "No," Riyad said again.

"How long you been working out here?"

Riyad glanced behind him where other men were emerging from their trailers. A few wore the baseball caps with *JT Flooring* stitched in orange. He hoped he wouldn't be late for work and have to explain why to the site superintendent. "You mean in Watford?"

"In North Dakota, sir," the detective said.

Riyad knew to the exact hour how long he'd been there. "Uh, a year and a half, I think. I was in Fargo before here."

"Where'd you say you're from, sir?" This came from the second detective. He was also shorter than Riyad, but he had the build of a boxer—broad shoulders and a chest that narrowed to a tight waist. His neck was wide and comical underneath his shirt and tie. Both detectives were wearing jeans and boots.

"Near Chicago," Riyad told him.

"That's where you lived, sir," the first detective said. "What's your nationality?"

"I'm an American citizen," he told them.

The men looked at each other. He knew what they were really asking, but he wouldn't make it easy for them. The first one continued to press him: "Are your parents originally from this country, sir?"

Riyad shook his head. "They're Palestinian."

The second one wrote something down in a small notebook he pulled from a back pocket of his jeans. "Did you say from Pakistan?"

"No. From Palestine." Riyad wondered if they knew where that was.

"Are you Muslim?" the first one asked. He pronounced it as *mooz-lum.*

"Yes," Riyad said, though he hadn't ever been a practicing one. He fasted only a few days during Ramadan and that was only for show, to keep his mother from nagging him about haram. He didn't drink or eat pork, but he didn't pray five times a day, either. Still, he wanted to ask the detectives how this line of questioning was relevant to the murder of Letti Vega, and if they knew the first mosque in the United States had been established in Ross, a town less than a hundred miles northwest of Watford City. But, he knew it was better to keep his mouth shut and cooperate.

When a follow-up question didn't come, Riyad took it as his cue to move between them and walk over to his car. His beat-up Oldsmobile was covered in a layer of red dirt from the construction site where he worked—not the same site of the body. His Illinois plates were splattered, but still visible.

Five of the Mexicans from another crew had already taken off. Riyad believed they'd had nothing to do with Letti Vega's murder. Still, they didn't need Immigration sniffing around. The Watford City police didn't hassle the project managers over the sudden departure of half their crew; they, too, were confident the Mexicans weren't responsible. They'd been working for Dane & Holtz, Inc. much longer than Riyad and everyone knew they'd be back as soon as the dust settled. For a flash of a moment, he thought of taking off, too, but there wasn't anyone waiting for him in Illinois, and though no one was keeping him in North Dakota, he stayed. In spite of his innocence, his paranoia heightened like a skittish cat with perked-up ears.

He filled up at a gas station on Main Street. The sky was a grey blanket with wrinkles of dark clouds. Inside the food mart, he poured coffee in a Styrofoam cup and carefully placed the lid over it while other customers moved past him, trying not to touch him, it seemed to Riyad. The cashier didn't reply to his greeting, only offering a jerk of his chin.

Above rolls of lottery tickets, a small mounted TV flashed images of Letti Vega. Every news station showed the same two photographs: Letti Vega as a high school senior, her cap slightly tilted, yellow dangling tassel; and Letti Vega in a green dress with white polka dots, standing beside an old, brown-skinned woman—her grandmother, maybe. Riyad had only ever seen her in a denim shirt and tan pants, the uniform all the waitresses wore at Briggs, a restaurant off Highway 85 where she'd been working.

Riyad paid for his gas and coffee and pushed open the door, feeling a dozen pairs of eyes boring into his back. A drizzle came down and coated his thick hair. He climbed back in his car and wiped his head with some clean napkins he kept stashed in the glove compartment.

He drove past Briggs, slowing down to view the bustle of news reporters. The restaurant had a log cabin façade, its sides paved in red brick. A group of news reporters stood in the parking lot in clear plastic raincoats over their suits and dresses, holding umbrellas with one hand and a microphone in the other. He caught glimpses of vans with station signs from as far as Billings and New Town.

He pulled onto the construction site of Phase 2 of Autumn Creek, an apartment compound. His crew did the flooring for a hundred units. Rental buildings sprung up like concrete weeds in Watford City—another boom town. Riyad had worked in Dickinson and Fargo for the last year, on motels and senior living complexes. He wasn't sure where he'd go next once the construction ended. He'd been steadily pushing northwest, the country seemingly stretching out forever. Maybe Williston would turn up something for a few months. He figured Montana wouldn't be too friendly.

"Heard cops been askin' you questions," a voice behind him said. It was Tim O'Halloran, a veteran crewman from Minnesota who'd been ribbing Riyad the moment he arrived on the site last spring.

"Mind your own business," Riyad said over his shoulder.

O'Halloran sidled up close to him. He smelled like soap and sawdust. "You the killer, Ali Baba? Ha?" He gave a mean snort. The other white men laughed.

"What the fuck are you talking about, man?" Riyad snapped.

O'Halloran stopped walking. "Ah, what's he need with one chick?" he jeered. "They get a hundred virgins in heaven if they blow up a building."

Riyad turned around. "Fuck you, man!" He took a few steps towards O'Halloran. The other man was twice his size and weight, but Riyad had to make a move or it would be open season on him for the rest of job.

"Knock it off!" the site super yelled from a trailer yards away, waving his clipboard in the air. "We got work to do. Gather round." The men huddled in a semi-circle while the super ran down the weekly quota of tasks.

Henry Elbert stood beside Riyad. He had an interminable cough and was looking paler than usual. His eyes were red-rimmed. Riyad, Henry and another man, Nick Osman, shared a trailer, keeping their monthly expenses down while they finished the job. There'd been a fourth roommate, a guy from Jamestown—home of the World's Largest Buffalo—but he left three days after he'd arrived, muttering about missing his girlfriend and dog.

As the super rattled off notes from his clipboard, Henry fell into a fit of coughing.

"Fuck man," Tim O'Halloran complained. "You tryin' to get the rest of us sick? Go see a fuckin' doctor, why doncha?"

Henry skulked a few feet backwards, flicking his reddish-blonde hair, still damp from a shower. Most of the men showered before they went to sleep, but Henry took two: one in the morning and one immediately after work. He pressed his fist against his colorless lips and his body shuddered for the rest of the meeting. Riyad felt sorry for the guy. Henry Elbert was someone the other men disliked as much as they did him, "an Ay-rab come to the Wild West."

"Alright, that's it. Now get to work," the super ordered the crew, waving his clipboard in the air again.

Inside the third floor, Riyad fastened his knee guards and stooped to the cement floor. With his trowel, he applied the adhesive for each laminate panel in a circular motion. The repetition made him feel steady and calm, the tension from his confrontation with Tim O'Halloran seeping out of his muscles. He was glad to be working indoors, too. He remembered the crews in Fargo last winter who'd suffered subzero temperatures finishing a roof or putting up siding to meet their quota for the month.

He pulled off his sweatshirt, revealing the bright orange company shirt JT Flooring had given each employee. Rain poured the whole day, coating the new unit windows and blurring the outside.

* * *

Riyad hadn't been back to Briggs since the body was pulled from the hole. It was a saloon-style restaurant where the regular crews ate steak-burgers and drank beer for lunch and dinner. Riyad ate there once a week, sometimes alone and sometimes with Henry Elbert and Jesus Padilla, a Mexican he'd met back in Fargo. He'd given Riyad a lead on the job in Watford City.

They'd eaten at Briggs just two days before a Missing Person report was filed for Letti Vega. "I'm going to Florida," Henry had said over his fried chicken dinner. "Fuck the cold and dust. I'm going to get one of those wiener wagons by the beach. I'll be fucking made. I just need to save some more cash than I can blow this shithole." He cleared his throat, making a low guttural sound like an animal. An elderly couple seated at a nearby table had turned and grimaced at him.

Jesus was undocumented and didn't contribute much to the conversation of Florida and wiener wagons. His brown eyes roamed over Henry's face then past him and Riyad to the men whooping at the bar. Riyad couldn't read Jesus's face, but there was a glint of contempt in his eyes.

The three of them avoided sitting at the bar with men like Tim O'Halloran and his buddies who turned even more territorial, their elbows hanging off the polished counter, each of them loudly vying for the attractive bartender's attention. One time the restaurant manager had to be called to settle down O'Halloran's crew when one of them tried to climb over the bar.

Riyad preferred a booth when it was only him and Henry. Jesus occasionally returned to the trailer park with the other Mexicans who were smart about their paychecks and packed their own lunches. Back in Fargo, when Riyad had asked him about kids, Jesus had raised three fingers and proudly grinned. Riyad wondered if it was easy to forget about them and legal papers and a wife when you were chomping down on a steak-burger. Maybe that's why Jesus spent time with him and Henry. Everyone had something—or someone—to forget, even if it was just for a little while.

Briggs was open seven days a week. The interior was dimly lit with heavy lacquered wooden tables and high-backed booths. Heads of bison and deer and a brown and white speckled cow were mounted along the perimeter of the dining hall. Hanging above the hostess podium was a framed "Code of the West" in old-fashioned Western typeface. The walls were lined with WANTED posters of real outlaws including the Dalton Brothers, a trio of bank and train robbers, and a woman named Belle Starr, a celebrated horse thief.

Riyad saw the same three or four waitresses every time he dined there. They huddled close to each other to gossip at the refreshment station, touching each other's shoulders, reaching over one another for a coffee mug or a bunch of plastic drinking straws.

Letti Vega usually served them during her shift, and if the hostess started to lead them away to another part of the restaurant, Henry would ask her to seat them in Letti's area, without mentioning her by name.

She wasn't like the other waitresses. She smiled politely and said hello then immediately took down their order. She spoke Spanish to Jesus when he had a question about an item. She never asked "How's it going, boys?" or "You almost finished Phase 2?" the way Emma Sue or Casey, the white waitresses, asked the construction men. Their faces were tanned year round and their pants were snug around their asses, not loose-fitting like Letti's. Her body was slender with small breasts and a short torso. They lingered at the tables where architects and PMs looked over blue prints, and they laughed long and heartily at the masculine quips.

Letti wore a light-pink polish on her short and clipped nails. The first time she'd served them, Riyad noticed something of a tattoo creeping out of the hem of her sleeve. It might have been a flower petal or the edge of a butterfly wing. When she was waiting for an order to come up, she smeared lip balm across her mouth and checked her cellphone.

The other men didn't seem to notice her. Except for Henry. He never said more than "please" and "thank you" and "what's the soup today?" but it was obvious to Riyad that he was enamored with Letti though she appeared to be less aware of him than she was of the other men who bellowed and knocked drinks on their tables. She performed her duties like she was inside a protective bubble. Others instinctively remained at bay, leaving her undisturbed.

Even Henry had left her alone, though Riyad could see words forming on his lips, anticipation shining in his eyes. When she brought their order, Henry only looked down at his food and nodded.

* * *

After work, he ate at Taco John's then drove south on Highway 85, gladder than usual for his Oldsmobile. Most of the crewmen didn't own transportation. He knew a few who had hitched all the way from Michigan and Iowa for work. The men had formed carpools; if anyone asked, he obliged them with a ride in the morning or dropped them off at the nearest bar after a long day. He never accepted offers for a free beer in return.

He drove past the oil fields where pump-jacks dipped into the ground like rocking horses. There was something painfully lonely to Riyad about the constant dipping—this quiet, uninterrupted motion reminding him that it didn't matter where he was in the county or state—life was unbroken. You had to put up with what you'd been dealt. Crews full of Mexican and white men showed up everyday, apartment buildings went up where desolate land had been. There'd be someone else to replace him in his trailer cot as soon as he was gone.

He pulled off near the Maah Dey Hey trail and watched the sunset. The first time he drove west from Fargo, the badlands took him by surprise, jagged buttes suddenly swelling around him and stratified valleys waking him from the torpor of a hundred miles of flat terrain. The highway was like a concrete serpent slinking through the hills of Watford City. The crew from Fargo suggested he stop at Theodore Roosevelt National Park to see the buffalo.

"You can only go six miles in," the park ranger had informed him. She was a middle-aged white woman with a round, pleasant face. "Erosion. You'll see the roadblocks." She had a map ready to hand him. "That will be twenty dollars, sir."

Riyad fished in his wallet. He'd cashed his last check from the Fargo job and all he had was a few hundred-dollar bills. "Can you break this?" He extended one out of his car window.

The ranger shook her head. "Can't help you with that." She gave him a map anyways and said, "You'll get us next time, sir. Enjoy."

It had been early May and the buffalo were molting, their fur hanging in patches from their flanks, looking less majestic than Riyad had imagined. He pulled off the path and watched a pair grazing several yards away. They chewed the new grass and snorted indifferently.

It was fall now, and the buffalos would be coated in fur again. A steady rain came down and Riyad turned off the wipers. A thin sheet covered his windshield. Next month was October and Phase 2 would be finished. He was glad Letti Vega's body hadn't been dumped on his site. Then he felt awful. A young girl was dead and all he could think about was completing a job so he could move on.

He took out his cellphone and listened to Marwa's message again. It was nearly two years ago and he still hadn't erased it.

"I'll wait another year, if you want. I deserve more, but I'll wait for you."

She had not intended to be unkind. It was a fact. Arabiyat like Marwa were accustomed to a certain lifestyle that he couldn't provide.

He imagined her holding her cellphone with one hand and rubbing the tip of her middle finger over the nail of her pointer finger like she did when she was thinking hard about something. The day before he left, they parked on the lakefront in Chicago, outside the Adler Planetarium where the view of the city skyline was the best. Marwa had looked at him but Riyad sensed she wasn't really seeing him. He wanted to reach over and kiss her eyelids shut and press his lips against her thick lashes. Instead he had gently squeezed her arm, pulling her out of a reverie of their life together.

When he was twelve years old, his father died of a blood clot in a prison in central Illinois. He'd been sentenced to twenty years for illegally cashing food stamps at his grocery store. His uncle and cousin were also convicted and still serving time. Riyad never drove a BMW or Range Rover like the other boys from school. He started working at fourteen, riding his bicycle to a gas station five miles from the cramped condo he, his older sister and his mother rented in Orland Hills.

Marwa lived on a two-acre lot with her family. It was a sprawling all-brick house with a circular driveway and a four-car garage. She drove a white Escalade with tinted windows from the dealership her father owned. So many things kept Marwa out of his league, but she was drawn to Riyad. Maybe it was the quiet way he moved among the other puffed-up guys, or maybe it was his inability to treat her badly, which most of the arabiyat would take as love.

"What will you do now?" she'd asked him. They watched people jogging and walking along Lake Michigan. In the distance, the movement of the gigantic Ferris wheel was imperceptible.

Marwa was graduating from UIC while he'd been working for a family-owned flooring business. That had given him enough experience for North Dakota.

He'd never been farther than Wisconsin, but he owned a car and he had a say over where he could go. His mother and sister had cried when he told them he was leaving. Their farewell felt more like an acknowledgement of failure than a herald of opportunity.

Riyad started the wipers, the horizon visible again in the thinning light.

He drove back to the trailer camp and parked his car next to a black Camaro that belonged to his roommate Nick. He unlocked the door of his trailer and climbed in. Nick was watching TV and thumbing through an auto magazine. He gave Riyad a look and shook his head in the direction of Henry's curled up body.

Sweat and farts permeated the trailer. Riyad pushed out a small window over the kitchen sink then squatted down next to Henry. "You okay, man?"

Henry cleared his throat, the low guttural sound muffled by his pillow. "Leave me alone."

Riyad stood and looked over at Nick who shook his head again. "Fine. I'm gonna wash up."

Before turning in, he sat on his cot and watched the nightly news with Nick. There was a twelve-inch TV screen fitted into a shelf at the opposite end of the trailer. New details on the murder revealed a young man who Letti Vega apparently had been seeing. He was filmed huddled under an umbrella, exiting the Watford City police station with a white man in a suit—his lawyer, no doubt. As reporters followed him to a waiting car, he kept his head down, his long brown hair obscuring his face.

A blonde news anchor stated, "Friends of Vega say they had no knowledge she had been involved with Johnny Lopez, a twenty-three-year old janitor at Good Christian Academy in nearby Charbonneau. Tonight, authorities say he is not being charged, only questioned. We'll have more on that case as further information becomes available. Now let's go to Tom Haverson to see what weather's in store for the Great Plains. Tom…"

Riyad watched Henry's cocooned body. It made no perceptible movement during this latest revelation.

"Good night," Riyad told Nick. He pulled the kitchen window shut.

"Night," Nick flicked off the TV and a light switch over his cot.

Wind hissed near the trailer door, the cold air penetrating the seams. Riyad turned over on his side and faced the wall. He was still awake when he heard a small whimper, but Riyad didn't sit up to check what it was. Instead, he pulled his blanket over his shoulders and soon he was asleep.

The next morning, Henry Elbert was gone. The detectives showed up again, this time talking to Nick and letting Riyad through without a word.

* * *

"These *gueros* are wasted, man," Jesus warned Riyad when he pulled onto the site. A light rain was falling and the orange construction flags flapped hard in the wind.

Riyad looked over at the management trailer. "Is the super here yet?"

Jesus shook his head under his jacket hood. "Don't know."

"Come on," Riyad said, his shoulders tightening. "Just ignore them." He nudged Jesus in the arm.

They walked toward the apartment building, away from Tim O'Halloran and a small crowd that had assembled around him. He was swaying on his heels, a bottle of Jim Beam in his hand. One of his buddies was trying to release it from his drunken grip. When O'Halloran caught sight of Riyad, he charged.

"It was you! You dirty sand-nigger!" Tim O'Halloran shouted, pushing Riyad in the chest. He stumbled backwards, tripping over a pallet of flooring panels.

"Fuck you!" Riyad shouted, pain tearing through his back. Jesus helped him to his feet and kept a hold of his arm, pulling him away.

"You terrorist fucker!" O'Halloran tried to push through the barricade of men holding him back. "Get the hell off me!" He teetered for a moment then steadied himself.

The super jumped out of a trailer. "You'd better calm down." He stood in front of O'Halloran with his hands up. "You quiet down or I'll call the cops."

"Call the fuckin' cops! You're lettin' a killer go!" O'Halloran yelled at him.

"Get him out of here before I have him locked up," the super instructed the men. "Let him sleep it off. And you tell him if he shows up with alcohol on the site again, he's fired."

O'Halloran suddenly turned limp at this threat and permitted the men to half-carry him to a pick-up truck. They drove off the site, a swirling dust of gravel in their wake.

The super walked over to Riyad. "You alright, son?"

The throbbing in his lower back had dulled, but a sharp pain shot through his legs when he took a step forward.

"You need to go to the hospital?"

Riyad shook his head. "I'll be fine," he said. Jesus helped him to a pile of mortar bags covered in tarp. He sat down in a sharp wince of pain.

"Take the morning off and see how you feel," the super instructed him.

By noontime, Riyad could barely stand in his trailer, let alone sit up on his cot. "Fuck," he muttered.

He called the super who drove him to McKenzie County Hospital where they gave him some painkillers and a cold compress and assured him it was nothing more than a mild sprained back—no permanent damage.

"Do you want to press charges?" the super asked him on the drive back to the trailer camp. His tone suggested he hoped there would be no more bad press on the construction site.

Riyad gazed out the window at the oil fields. Despite the rain, small fires blazed from gas flares. They looked like torches, strange beacons of something he could not name.

"No. I don't know," Riyad said. He was humiliated and in the worst pain he'd ever felt. "I'll think about it."

In the end, he decided not to press charges. He knew it wouldn't make friends of the other men, but he certainly couldn't afford any more enemies. When he returned to work several days later, no one acknowledged the gesture, but they left him alone.

Soon he was able to drive himself to work and the first chance he got he headed down Highway 85 at the end of his shift. Thunderstorms had gradually moved east, leaving the valleys looking electrified in the gray-blue dusk. He would miss this part of the country once Phase 2 was complete.

He pulled off the highway and turned off the ignition. He reclined the seat. A dull pain throbbed in his lower back, but it wasn't unbearable. His eyelids felt heavy and he closed them and rested his head against the cool glass of the driver's side window. At first, he didn't fight the images of Marwa and Letti Vega and Henry Elbert floating across his mind.

Then something stabbed at his heart and he opened his eyes. Maybe Henry realized even a wiener wagon was too big, and Letti Vega was the final straw. One more thing he couldn't have.

Riyad felt nauseous. He quickly turned the ignition to open his window. He breathed in the badland air. His head cleared again and he steadied his gaze on the sun's descent. It cast long and wide shadows in the valley and over the browning steppe.

Maybe there was still a chance to leave. He couldn't go back to Illinois—the land was too flat. Not Florida, either. Too humid. Maybe California—a town near the ocean. A new calm washed over him. The sun had finally set leaving a brushstroke of pink and orange across the horizon. After a few more comatose minutes he pulled back on the highway.

The trailer park was quiet. Most of the men were out drinking or asleep.

Riyad parked his car between two pick-up trucks and climbed out. He looked at his trailer, wondering how far Henry had gotten.

The first blow to the back of his head brought an explosion of white-hot light beneath his eyelids. The second one brought darkness.

Tim O'Halloran lowered the lead pipe and nudged the slumped body with the tip of his boot. "Should've stayed where he come from."

It was barely a whisper, but the two other men heard him and nodded, though neither of them had ever really known where that place was.

Shisha Love

You used to smoke the shisha after a plate of your mother's stuffed cabbage, or at Souk on Taylor Street, together with your girlfriends. Now you smoke it when you're waiting for him to come home, after he's gone down on his Lithuanian girlfriend. She has a thin nose and blue eyes. You smell her on his breath—a scent strangely like papaya-flavored tobacco you smoked once.

His parents threatened to disown him if he married her, so he married you—a respectable arabiya who wears fashionable hijab and attends the Bridgeview Mosque fundraisers. You pretend you don't know about that woman and wait until he comes around and sees you can be just as sexy as her—and be his whore, too—though you've given birth twice in three years and your dimpled thighs and ass are not as firm as they used to be. Your stomach is no longer taut, your shriveled navel has lost its allure. Still, every night you loosen your long, wavy hair from a tight bun, letting it spill over your shoulders like the licorice juice your centenarian grandfather, Siddo Jaddallah, drinks once a day in the summertime.

In your eggplant and sage-hued kitchen, you prepare the shisha. You stand at the granite island and scoop the moist and fragrant black cherry tobacco from its round metal container. You store it in the back of the refrigerator so Musa doesn't get his plump hands on it when he's looking for his Jell-O Pudding cups. The coolness sharpens the flavor of the tobacco like menthol in a cigarette filter.

With a tablespoon, you delicately pack the tobacco into the small bowl. If you listen closely, you can hear it squish down into place, like footsteps in mud. You cut a square of aluminum foil to cover the tobacco bowl then pierce the surface with a toothpick. Tiny holes for ventilation emit shame and failure, opening up like pores in your olive skin, though everyone tells you men will be men.

He doesn't beat you, he doesn't gamble—Allah forbid.

What arrabi man is perfect?

He's a great father, Alhamdulillah.

He married you, after all. Count your blessings.

In the kitchen sink, you let the faucet run cold and fill up the glass water-base, shaped like an oversized perfume bottle—a stolen relic from the chambers of a concubine in a sultan's palace. The glass is the color of an emerald and embellished with gold laurels.

You attach the copper stem to the water-base then screw the tobacco bowl to the top of the stem, and connect the braided hose to its side. You wrap your fingers around the shaft, cradling the base in your other hand as you carry the shisha out to the balcony and carefully set it on the concrete floor. You sit on one of the wrought iron pub chairs—a pair with a matching table that you knew would be perfect for this space—to watch the cars whiz past on Wolf Road, and listen to the wailing horn of an evening commuter train as it deposits stragglers returning to the suburbs. You hear the crackling of their heels on gravel. They walk quickly to their cars, unlock the door, and speed out of the parking lot. The city skyline is a vague memory.

With tiny steel tongs, you lift two round charcoals from a red box called "Three Kings" with a picture of the Magi on camels, facing the horizon. You position the coals on the foil-covered tobacco bowl and ignite them with a butane mini-torch; sparks dance across their spheres.

As you wait for the coals to blaze into small setting suns, you head back inside and lean against the door where Musa and the baby sleep. Lena has finally suspended her two a.m. feedings—though you never really minded being pulled out of a half-empty bed. You slide the patio door shut behind you and settle on your chair, checking your cell phone for a text that he's on his way.

You look up as the night sky fills with stars. A breeze rushes across your cheeks and you take off your hijab because no one can really see your bare head from the street. You want to feel the coolness seep into your thick strands of your hair and caress your scalp. The charcoals flare up from the breeze like lava rocks then die down as hope tends to do.

You lift the hose and instinctively wipe the mouthpiece across your thigh even though you're the only who smokes from this it. If he were there, he'd ask for a disposable mouth tip despite other fluids you exchange, twice this month. He insists he doesn't want to catch a cold.

The first drag is supreme. It's like opening a valve and something more essential, more desperate than oxygen saturates your lungs. These spongy basins become heavy, but it is an exquisite weight to bear, not a load of humiliation that makes your shoulders stoop a little when people greet you at eid celebrations, their low voices fringed with pity.

With each successive draw from the hose, the water gurgles in the emerald base until you release your lips from the tip. Your mouth is piquant and your lips full of promise as they suck in the black cherry smoke. It coats your teeth like a sugary moss. You lean your head back and exhale—rapture—wondering if the Lithuanian woman has already come in his mouth.

In one swallow of black cherry smoke, you, too, experience all the flavors of love until the shisha's final embers fade into night.

Masculine Verbs

Emad stood poised with his slingshot, aiming at a cypress tree with wide-fanning branches. The sky was gray and the air was hazy with humidity. Lizards skittered in and out of thorn bushes.

The other boys respectfully waited for him to make his shot, their faces dirt-streaked and moist. The thick elastic band grew taut as Emad gripped the orange-red jagged rock and released. A few branches rustled, but nothing fell from the tree.

Tamer, the shortest in the bunch, had trouble keeping up his excessively large jeans. He nagged his brother Hatim for a turn to hold the slingshot.

"Stingy bastard," Tamer said, shoving his brother in the shoulder. He had a shock of white hair like a rabbit's foot sprouting from the crown of his head. It had turned that way after the yahood dragged their oldest brother away in the middle of a night two years ago. One of the soldiers had kept an automatic rifle aimed at Tamer and Hatim's mother the whole time.

Emad carried a slingshot his brother Khamis had given him and it was the only thing he did not have to share with anyone. Still, he gave it to Tamer when his brother Hatim refused him a turn.

Hatim poked Tamer hard in the stomach with his slingshot. "Shut up and shoot," he told his brother.

Tamer blew the dust off of a small rust-colored rock and positioned it in the elastic band. His rock skidded far above the cypress tree and the other boys teased him.

Emad and the other boys had been coming to shoot at birds with their slingshots—mostly warblers and sand grouse—sometimes trapping blue and green bee-eaters in nets to sell at the souk. On the crest of the small mountain, they could see a settler in a watchtower and signs in Hebrew secured to barbed wire.

When Emad readied himself again to shoot, a car appeared in the wadi. It rolled to a stop among old newspapers with yellowed visages of angry protestors and Hillary Clinton shaking hands with a timid diplomat.

The young man and woman drove into the wadi every Thursday afternoon—except during Ramadan. The tires of the Mercedes Benz crunched over rocks and plastic bottles discarded in the clearing.

The first time the sleek black car drove into the valley, Emad could tell it was a man from the Palestinian Authority—the sulta. The license plate numbers were painted red and on the bottom corner of the rear window was the emblem of the sulta—a golden falcon, its profile facing left like a hieroglyphic. Sitting beside the man was always the same woman with brown straight hair and dark sunglasses that covered half of her face. Some days she wore a coiled bun, but most days it settled around her shoulders like a scalloped curtain.

Emad and the other boys trotted towards the car. The man from the sulta poked his head out of his window as they drew closer.

"Loolad! Boys!" he called out. "Get out of here! Go play somewhere else!" Emad could see light-brown hair sprouting from the unbuttoned collar of the man's fancy shirt. It was the same light color of his head and up close, Emad saw a spattering of freckles on the bridge of the man's nose. Though he was seated, his shoulders were broad and his biceps were tight under his iron-pressed shirt when he waved them away. The man looked like he took showers every day and applied cologne that faintly wafted in the breeze outside the fancy car.

"We were here first, man!" Hatim had asserted. He was twelve years old like Emad. He brazenly gripped the doorframe of the driver's side and peered in at the man and woman, craning his head to scrutinize the backseat of the car. "What do you two plan on doing here alone?" Hatim demanded.

"Wallak, you little bastard!" the man had yelled. "Mind your own business!" He pushed Hatim in the chest and the boy stumbled backwards into Emad. The man pretended to unlock his car door, and Emad and the boys flew off, behind some kumquat trees, laughing and hooting,.

They watched the movement in the car from the vista of the passenger side. The man from the sulta held the woman's chin in his hand and stroked her hair. He removed her glasses and pulled her shirt up over her bra, but Emad saw that he never took it off. After a while, the man kissed her cheek then guided her head to his crotch and leaned back.

Emad and the boys just gawked at the car until the man jerked and moaned. The woman's head appeared again and she wiped her mouth against her forearm. After the man cleaned himself up and tossed a crumbled ball of tissue paper out of the window, they drove away.

The next week the Mercedes Benz appeared again and the man from the sulta offered each boy a shekel to go away. Emad had tucked his coin deep in his front pocket, his head teeming with gifts of cigarettes for his brother Khamis and ice cream for himself. He and the other boys hid behind the same tree and watched until the woman's head resurfaced. If anyone had stumbled upon the car they might have thought the man from the sulta was merely taking a nap.

The car was right on time again today.

"Here come the lovebirds," Hatim jeered. "Time to get paid."

Emad and Tamer stood awkwardly at the hood of the car, Tamer fingering the car's chrome emblem. The man beeped the horn and shook his finger at Tamer. He returned his attention to Hatim who negotiated the terms for the couple's privacy in exchange for money. Tamer stood close to Hatim, his arm slung lazily over his brother's shoulder as he listened.

Emad could tell the man was impressed by Hatim and his audacity. Earlier, the boys had decided to push for an increase in wages. Emad watched his friend's easy manner as Hatim tapped the roof of the car and conveyed their latest demand to the man from the sulta. Emad never spoke more than necessary and only to his friends. He wished he had the same courage as Hatim.

In the passenger seat, the woman kept touching her sunglasses. The lenses were darker than usual because there was no sun. She appeared uncomfortable as she dipped her head down towards her cellphone and tapped buttons on its screen. If Emad ever passed her at the souk and she was wearing hijab, he probably would not recognize her.

"Do you think he cums in her mouth?" Tamer asked the other boys as they sat on their haunches behind the trees.

"I'd cum on her tits," Hatim said, rolling a rock between his hands. "Whores love that."

Emad didn't say anything though he had conjured several fantasies over the last few weeks when he lay on his back on his floor mattress. Everyone was asleep, except for Khamis who lost twenty pounds when he was in prison for a year and had never regained them. His brother chain-smoked cigarettes in the only other room of their cinderblock beit. The television always played on mute. His mother lay on a thin mattress on the kitchen floor a few feet away from him, sometimes mumbling as she dreamt. His sister Keeyan, the oldest, slept perpendicular to him so that her feet sometimes touched Emad's when she stirred.

That woman in the car did not quite look like a whore to him—although Emad was not entirely sure what a whore might look like.

"If she were my sister, she'd be dead," Hatim said, pointing an imaginary gun at the car with one squinted eye. He drew a bead then discharged, his hand jerking back as though a real bullet had ripped from a barrel.

"Who'd want to screw your sister?," Emad joked.

Hatim was unsure whether to accept this as an insult or not. Tamer rubbed his ear and waited for his brother to respond.

"Kuss immak," Hatim finally said. "Screw your mother."

They all laughed this time and jumped to their feet and raced each other back to the camp.

* * *

The stench of sewage in the refugee camp was like rotten cabbage and it filled every pore and fiber of Emad's body. He closed the metal security door behind him when he entered his beit and the odor of the majarri still clung to him like a gauzy veil.

"Emad!" It was his sister Keeyan. She was home early from the medical clinic in Ramallah where she assisted nurses. She was the only one working since his father left them. "Wash up quickly! We need to talk."

He rushed to the tiny washroom. His mother had wrapped an old dingy towel around the stem of the toilet to capture leaking water. The rim of the toilet bowl, which his mother vigorously scrubbed every morning, was stained brown. Emad flushed, hoping the chain would not come undone, and washed his hands.

He gazed at himself in the mirror, opening his mouth and examining his tonsils. There was a long crack in the glass that stopped abruptly below his right eye in the reflection. Several months ago, it had stretched to his right cheek, and a year ago it barely reached his jawline. He knew it would not be too long before the crack in the mirror split his entire face in two.

Emad put his ear to the bathroom door before pulling out the coins and setting them on the chipped sink. He knelt down and removed a piece of tile in the floor and lifted an old tin box for bandages, wrapped in cellophane. He and the boys had received enough money to pay an electric bill for their parents or to purchase shawarma sandwiches in town. He dropped the coins into the tin box and they rattled like heavy raindrops against the sheet metal roof of his beit. He wrapped the box again in the crinkly cellophane and returned it to his hiding place.

At the square table flushed against one wall of the kitchen, his sister and mother were drinking tea with sage. A pot of mlookhiya and chicken simmered on the stove. The aroma of the leafy stew mingled with starchy rice.

Khamis wasn't home.

After she downed her glass and placed it in the sink, Keeyan pumped a small cloud of foamy hand sanitizer into her palm. It had a label containing words in Arabic, Hebrew and a language Emad didn't know. She brought bottles home from the clinic and insisted everyone apply the stuff as often as possible—except for Khamis, to whom she barely spoke. She inspected Emad's fingernails once a week before permitting him to go to bed.

Emad watched as Keeyan pressed her palms together and rubbed them in small circles before spreading the foam over the back of her hands, massaging her fingers and knuckles. Her body was shaped like plump fig, bottom-heavy with a narrow torso.

"Sayida Muna came into the clinic today," Keeyan said. She was Emad's science teacher at Ramallah School for Boys.

Keeyan hadn't taken off her hijab yet and it was wrapped tightly around her head as though it were second skin. Emad was used to seeing it frame her face than without it, and her complexion was light like his mother's. Emad was dark like his father from what he could tell in a few photographs of him that his mother had tucked away in a broken-down bureau in the room where he slept. His mother took one of Khamis's old school copybooks and wedged it under one side so it would not tilt. When he was younger, he would stand on his tiptoes and lean over the top drawer, examining the photographs without taking them out. He'd spread them above a layer of his mother's cotton underwear and prayer clothes. His face was round like his father's and they shared the same coal-black hair like a mist had permanently settled over it.

"She says she hasn't seen you for a week," Keeyan continued, her hands gripping her plump forearms on the table.

Emad's mother sat with one elbow propped on her palm, the other hand pressed against her cheek. "Where have you been, yamma?" his mother earnestly asked. Crow's feet were deeply stamped around her eyes and her lids drooped with resignation. She looked at Emad as though she were already grieving another lost son.

There were only two chairs in the kitchen so he stood before the women, his face flushed with guilt and a tinge of anger when he thought of the other boys, believing they did not have to endure an interrogation concerning their whereabouts.

"Well? Where have you been?" Keeyan demanded. She placed a finger inside her hijab to scratch a spot above her ear and he wondered why she did not simply unfasten the fabric to free her head now that she was indoors.

He still did not answer. He knew Keeyan would give up after a few more tries. His eyes dropped to the corner of the kitchen floor where a cockroach was trying to squeeze into a crack in the wall. It tried several times before abandoning its plan and scuttled alongside the wall for a new route.

"Your education is important, ya Emad," his sister declared. "I wish you could see that and make better choices."

It sounded like she was repeating what Sayida Muna had told her. He imagined that conversation and the way she sounded different from the other female teachers like Sayida Amal or Sayida Nabiha. Sayida Muna was born in the United States, and she had an accent that Emad envied. It was an accent that instantly alerted people she was only a visitor—a temporary guest—with a passport stamped with an Israeli insignia because it was far more convenient to travel through Ben Gurion than wait hours to cross at the Allenby Bridge in Jordan.

When she spoke, she did not always roll her r's and she sometimes forgot to conjugate a verb according to the masculine rule when she scolded a boy. He joined the rest of the class as it roared in laughter, yet he was secretly envious of such slips in language.

"You must return to school, yamma," his mother said, gently pulling a tuft of hair near his forehead and drawing him closer to her. He could smell the fresh garlic in her fingertips that she had minced and added to the stew. "Tayib?"

Emad silently nodded.

"Alright then," his mother said. "Let's wait for Khamis just a little while more and then we'll eat." She hoisted herself from the table and lowered the flame under the pot on the stove. "Ya rubbi, give me strength."

Outside the small barred window, the neighbor's son was cursing members of his family for drinking the last bottle of cola.

* * *

On the verge of falling asleep that night, Emad heard low mumbling coming from the sitting room. He soundlessly rose from the floor mattress,careful not to tap his sister's heaving body. He poked his head out the bedroom door. The moonlight shone on a large framed scripture from the Qu'ran. It was "Surat Yaseen," the one his mother had recited each night for a year when Khamis was in prison.

Khamis was reclined across the lumpy couch, his head tilted back against a worn armrest on one end. One arm hung limply off the side and a lit cigarette dangled between his rough fingers. A metal ashtray rested on his brother's stomach. His other arm covered his eyes as though a bright light had penetrated the near-darkness of the room. His chest was bony and hollow like a bird's, and his limbs were deeply tan and ashy.

"Khamis? Are you okay?" Emad whispered. He knelt down beside his brother. He looked over at his mother as she mumbled something and turned over on the kitchen floor.

"All I smell is that sewage," Khamis said, barely audible. "All the shit and piss running outside the beit, between every other beit. It doesn't matter where I go, that majarri flows inside me like my own blood. I stink of it.

"What are you talking about?" Emad grew frightened and glanced again at his mother, hoping she would wake up.

"Get away from me," Khamis muttered. "I stink."

"I don't smell anything," Emad said. He touched his brother's knee.

In a flash, Khamis grabbed him by the shoulder, still clutching his cigarette. Crushed butts spilled from the ashtray.

"You son of a whore," Khamis shouted in his face.

His breath was gamy and hot and his eyes were wide and maniacal like the Japanese cartoons Emad watched when he grew tired of playing outside with the boys. Emad tried to wrench himself free and the tip of the cigarette singed his neck.

"For the love of the Prophet," his mother cried out. "Khamis! Leave your brother alone!" She was standing behind Emad, trying to unclench Khamis's grip.

He finally released Emad and stubbed out his cigarette in the toppled ashtray. "Inshallah, this whole place crumbles to hell," Khamis said quietly, sliding into a pair of leather sandals and kicking the steel door open.

Emad clutched his neck where Khamis had burned him with his cigarette. He heard his brother's footsteps crackle down the gravel road and what sounded like a stone being kicked into a tiny puddle of water.

When he woke up very early the next morning, he found Khamis sleeping on the couch. One side of his face was bruised and the knuckles of his right hand were cut and smeared with dried blood.

"Yamma," Emad gently nudged his mother. "Wake up."

"Aywa, yamma," she said drowsily. She sat up and rubbed her eyes.

"Look at Khamis," Emad told her.

His mother grabbed the edge of the sink and hoisted herself to her feet. She wore two dishdashas to stay warm each night and the hem of a purple one as dark as an eggplant reached past her ankles, dragging when she walked.

"*Yeeeee!* What have you done to yourself, yamma!" his mother cried. "Khamis! Wake up! Were you in a fight?"

"Leave me alone," Khamis mumbled, curling his body into a ball. He covered his head with both hands.

"Ya rubbi, how much more can I stand!" his mother pleaded.

Keeyan woke up and stood next to Emad, her hand squeezing his shoulder. He could feel she wanted to say something, to intervene so that their mother could be spared distress. But Keeyan said nothing, watching along with him as the light of dawn broke through the barred window and cast a soft glow over Khamis's body. He looked like he was nestled inside of an egg.

"Get ready for school, yamma," his mother wearily instructed Emad. "Your brother's fine. Inshallah khair."

"Go on," Keeyan said, nudging him. "Sayida Muna expects to see you today and the rest of the week."

Emad dressed and grabbed his backpack. Keeyan slipped past him in the tiny hall cupping a glass of tea with both hands. In the kitchen, his mother had spread creamy yogurt in pocket bread and cut it in half for Emad to eat on his way to school. He would take the other half for lunch. She gave him a plastic bag with the sandwich and a guava.

"Do well in school, yamma," she said, mussing his hair.

Emad smoothed it back into place and headed out the door. He walked to the end of the gravel road where it opened to Sharafa Street and waited for Hatim and Tamer. Debris littered the road: soda cans and dirty diapers, old long-distance calling cards and empty cigarette cartons.

"Salaam," Hatim said, a cigarette tucked behind his ear. He ate a fragrantly ripe banana and tossed the peel over his shoulder. "I heard your brother was in a fight last night with Hussein."

Emad shrugged. He didn't know anything.

"Does he know how to box?" Tamer asked, eating his own banana. He had peeled it down to the stem, and it turned mushy between his fingers as he took bites.

"His knuckles had blood on them," Emad told them.

Hatim nodded wisely. "That's from throwing punches. Good for him. Some of these harra boys can't fight unless they have a stick."

Tamer wiped his hands on the back of his blue uniform slacks.

"Ya ihmar!" Hatim scolded. "Mama just washed those for you, you donkey!" He shoved his brother.

Tamer's cheeks flushed and he shoved his brother back, but with less conviction. "Why do you care, you dog?"

Hatim ignored him and they walked the rest of the way to school in silence.

In Sayida Muna's class, they were learning about tectonic plates. When she saw Emad, she nodded at him and seemed pleased. She asked him to assist him with a demonstration.

"You see, ya loolad," Sayida Muna explained, her voice louder than necessary. She wore a red-and-white checkered hijab and a form-fitting black dress with long sleeves. Her eyebrows were thin and arched and she wore kohl and light lip-gloss. "These bricks represent plates beneath the earth's surface." She was holding one against another she had given to Emad. "When they rub together, friction is created. Go ahead and rub it as hard as you can, Emad."

His classmates snickered and lowered their heads in their folded arms.

"Rub it harder, ya Emad," Hatim called from the back.

"Bas, ya, Hatim!" Sayida Muna warned. "Or I'll have another word with your mother. Now be still!"

When a few flakes broke off the bricks, Emad was congratulated and dismissed to his desk. For the rest of the period, he watched Sayida Muna's lips form her words, hearing nothing but unintelligible sounds. He daydreamed about earthquakes and how severe one had to be—perhaps a magnitude of six or seven—to completely shatter his home or to swallow up the mokhayam, leaving only a tangle of cinderblock wires like a nest of vipers.

At supper, Emad tried not to stare at Khamis. There was a welt on his brother's cheek like a slimy leech. His knuckles were swollen, too, and Emad could tell they hurt as Khamis ate his bowl of addas on the couch. The lentil soup dripped from the spoon as Khamis tried to hold it steady. His mother and sister ate at the table, Keeyan chatting about her day at the clinic. Emad sat on his mother's mattress and tried not to spill his soup.

Before prison, Khamis and Emad would sit together on the couch and eat side by side and watch television, mostly international soccer and popular Arabic talent shows. Now Emad stole glimpses of his brother whose eyes were on the muted television screen. The accompanying sound eerily echoed through the open window from Um Amjad's flat next door where the same channel was playing. The addas was warm and soft like bits of moistened tissue paper in his mouth and cumin lingered on his tongue after he swallowed spoonfuls of the lentil soup. A few of the children ran in and out of Um Amjad's beit, drowning out the newscaster's voice reporting on Al Jazeera. Emad continued to watch his brother who ate the addas with slow, deliberate scoops, letting it slosh around his mouth before swallowing.

"She's a lazy loudmouth," Keeyan was telling his mother. "I'm always one step behind her, wiping down the sinks and toilets a second time. I'm ready to go to the head nurse." His sister popped an olive in her mouth and chewed until Emad saw the pit emerge between her lips like a small pebble.

His mother listened and nodded, ladling more addas into Keeyan's bowl despite her protests. She craned her neck to check his bowl and he looked up at her from the mattress and shook his head before she could offer him more. His mother looked at Khamis. Emad waited to see if his brother could resist the weight of his mother's stare. He was successful, keeping his eyes on the screen.

Outside the flat next door, a child knocked over a tin can and dashed into the beit. Um Amjad stood at the threshold scolding whoever had carelessly knocked over her makeshift pot of spearmint stalks.

* * *

On a bright morning, he put on his uniform and grabbed his backpack with his slingshot in it, and he said goodbye to his mother. He closed the metal door behind him and sprinted down the road. Hatim and Tamer were waiting for him, but they were not in uniforms or carrying backpacks.

"Won't your mother know we're cutting school?" Emad asked them.

"She sleeps until salat el thuhr, then she takes another nap after she prays," Tamer explained, looking at his brother.

Hatim walked ahead of them, tapping his cigarette between puffs. Tamer rubbed the back of his head and did not say anything else.

They did not hit anything that morning except for a stray dog that whimpered from a shot to its hind leg. It scampered away before the boys could chase it. The sun had begun to beat down on them and they flapped their shirts against their chests to raise a breeze. The black car appeared and the boys received their shekels and retired under the cypress tree, lying close together in a narrow shade. By noon, the space of shade was wider as the tree branches shielded them from the sun and they could spread out comfortably. They talked with their eyes closed.

"Did your brother find a job, yet?" Hatim asked. The sound of his friend's voice came to Emad as through a helium balloon, dull and warped.

"No," Emad said. He was not sure if Khamis had been searching for work. What could Khamis even do? he wondered.

Before prison, his brother was only a month from taking the towjeehi secondary examinations. His mother had begged him to stay home when his class planned a demonstration in Jerusalem. He was arrested along with three other boys from the camp. It took a few days for his mother and sister to figure out where Khamis was being detained. He was convicted of conspiracy and sentenced to a year in prison.

Emad wondered what he had been doing that whole time—did he read or watch television? Did he play football like he did with the harra boys on Friday afternoons. They set up goal posts with empty oversized tin cans of pickles, and Khamis kicked the ball into the goal and no one could stop him.

A nest of baby warblers twittered high in the cypress tree, and underneath the boys sat in silence, Tamer and Hatim flipping their coins with their thumbs. The hood of the black car gleamed in the sunlight.

Emad felt hot and uneasy. He pinched the coins in his pocket and thought of his mother and sister. He imagined Khamis sprawled on the lumpy couch with nowhere to go, no work to be had.

As the woman's head descended into the man's lap, Emad suddenly leapt up like a warbler safely averting a rock jetting from a slingshot. He ran towards the car and gripped the window frame of the driver's door, breathing hard.

The woman jerked her head and sat up straight as a board in the passenger seat, fumbling to disguise her face with her sunglasses.

"What is it?" the man from the sulta asked, annoyed by the interruption. He covered his crotch. "What can I do for you, my brother?"

"You're not my brother," Emad said quietly. He was not sure he had uttered a word except that the woman turned to look at him.

He could discern the shape of her eyes beneath the dark glasses, could guess their color if he focused hard. He detected mango-flavored tobacco inside the car. Emad wondered if they had just come from Muntazat El Bireh where they had been smoking hookahs between sips of thick coffee. The man's hairline glistened with sweat and the woman's was tied back today in a tight bun. Her face was smooth and fair, her lips the pencil-drawn shape of a bird in flight, arced and perfect. His sister Keeyan had his mother's lips, softly outlined like someone had accidentally smudged them. Her hair was also darker than the woman in the car, streaks of blonde swirling in her bun.

In his peripheral vision, he saw Hatim and Tamer edge closer. A dog barked from the direction of the settler's watchtower and Emad imagined it standing sentry against the mokhayam boys who occasionally slung rocks at it.

The man from the sulta looked up at him quizzically. The man reached out to touch Emad's arm, but changed his mind. The woman kept her hands in her lap. Near her feet were a few cartons of cigarettes, the brand his brother Khamis smoked. He purchased a carton each week from the money Keeyan left on the counter for him. He would ration one pack a day from the freezer where he kept his cigarettes fresh. There were also empty water bottles with Hebrew labels scattered by the woman's sandaled feet.

"What do you want?" the man asked him.

The first punch to the man's jaw was painful like the time Emad's hand got caught under the weight of a crate of oranges he carried home for his mother from the souk. He had tripped in his haste and the pinewood scraped his fingers, opening tiny flaps of skin like eyelids. Now, his knuckles connected with the man's nose and he heard a slight crunching sound. Emad's fists were like mallets against nails, pounding the man's face, neck and shoulders. He wondered if his brother Khamis had felt the same excruciating throbbing of his knuckles from the other night when he returned home with gash under his eye. And if it had felt just as satisfying.

It felt like all the air inside of the car had been sucked into a vacuum and he could hear very little beyond the hysterical beating of his heart. He continued to punch the man from the sulta. Sometimes his fists slammed into the packed shoulder muscles, sometimes into the soft cartilage of ears. He had stopped aiming for the face and simply hit as much of the man's body as he could. The man from the sulta shoved him back a few times, but Emad slapped the awkwardly extended arm away from his chest and relentlessly punched. The man tried to grab Emad's wrists, but his body was lodged between his seat and the steering wheel, restricting his ability to hold onto Emad for more than a few seconds. He pulled at Emad's hair and his fingernails scraped Emad's cheeks.

The shrieks of the woman penetrated the space and Emad was being pulled away by Hatim who never let his brother use his slingshot and by Tamer whose white hair would never again be brown.

They flung him to the ground and he scrambled to his feet and dug in his pockets for the coins. Before dashing away, he whipped them against the windshield of the car and they clinked and danced off the hood. The man from the sulta was holding his bloodied nose and cursing. Emad could hear him commanding the other boys to fetch the coins. It would have been enough for a few dozen bags of freshly baked bread.

In the Event

Colin was in his gnawing stage. He tugged at the collar of his "Astronauts Need Their Space" T-shirt with his teeth, a damp circle of saliva slowly expanding on the yellow fabric. Samah, his classroom aide, was grateful he'd skipped head-thumping with his fist which she could never get used to despite all reassurances from Colin's mother that it did not physically hurt him.

The other boy who'd entered the classroom lowered his gun and laid it on the round table next to the tub of markers, his fingers still laced around it. He was no longer aiming it at her and Colin. Colin's breathing became less labored and he pressed his body close to Samah. He didn't hold her hand though she kept it flat and open between them. They huddled in the corner of Miss Taylor's classroom, the other boy sitting across from them, his shoulders slumped.

On any other day, when Colin grew agitated, Samah never directly touched him, but she gently led him away from the other special needs children and through an adjoining door where he could take a "time-out" in Miss Taylor's classroom. That's what they had been doing when the shots rang out in the hallway.

Moments before, Miss Taylor had gone to the mailroom to make photocopies of the task calendar for May and hadn't returned.

Samah had ordered Colin to the corner beside the Word Wall and quickly locked the door and shut the lights. The roller blinds were always down to minimize external stimuli for the children. She'd done everything she was instructed to do in the event of a crisis according to a police liaison who'd visited the Woodrow Wilson Middle School last fall. During his presentation, some of the staff had been chatting quietly with their neighbors in the small auditorium seats, several checking their texts, and others grading worksheets. Samah had sat completely alert, the mention of "perpetrator" sinking something deep in her stomach.

With icy fear, Samah realized she'd forgotten to lock the second door that connected the two classrooms. But it was too late. She and Colin watched as the other boy came through the adjoining door. When it swung closed behind him, Samah could see pairs of legs crisscrossing each other on the floor, blood pooling beneath them.

She knew Colin saw it, too, and instead of shrieking he'd seemed to comprehend the gravity of the situation and began to sway back and forth on his haunches, but he didn't make a sound.

A cacophony of stampeding feet and busted down doors made the quiet of the classroom even more palpable. Samah listened to the gnashing of Colin's teeth and the deep humming sound he made. Sirens wailed outside. A soft drizzle tapped at the windows. Colin's class was scheduled for an outdoor excursion to identify spring flowers in the community garden Ms. Shepard's 7th grade science class planted last September. There would be dahlias and tulips, yellow trillium and daffodils, but the rain had kept them indoors today.

Samah and Colin sat still in the corner, their arms grazing. The other boy looked around the classroom and Samah knew it was the first time he'd been in there, and in any other circumstance, he'd be excited to tell his friends what Self-Contained was like, how they had toys and easels, and jars with Twizzlers. But Samah realized the other boy didn't have friends, that perhaps there was no one besides his mother or a brother or sister who'd listen and smile sadly at him when he came home. She didn't know his name though she'd seen him coming out of Mr. Leonard's 8th grade homeroom a few times a week.

The other boy had not uttered a word to them until Colin's humming became high-pitched like a violin's frenzied notes.

"Is he a retard, or something?" the other boy said to Samah. The gun's barrel made slight clicking sounds against the top of the table and he sat up in the chair. She could see he was trying hard to keep his hand steady. His face scrunched up as though something had suddenly struck him and Samah thought he might start crying and maybe she'd be able to coax the gun out of his hand. His blonde hair was matted with sweat; he wore a brown faded jacket too large for him and the pockets bulged.

"He's autistic," Samah told the other boy, surprised at the calm in her voice. She inserted a finger inside her hijab, above her ear—an unconscious habit. The hair near her temple was damp with sweat. "He's very smart. Probably smarter than most of adults here." She shouldn't have said that. Colin repeated almost everything he witnessed. Her chest fluttered. She wouldn't care what he told the faculty as long as they made it out.

Colin's humming dropped again and he continued to chew the collar of his T-shirt. His eyes were glued on the other boy.

Meenshan Allah, Samah prayed, *please don't make him shoot you, for the love of God.* She'd whispered to him to remember the wormholes.

Colin nodded and pressed into her. When she'd first started at Woodrow Wilson Middle School, she was worried about being an aide in SC, as they called it. Maram and Omar, her children, were grown up, in graduate school and starting careers. Boredom seeped into her mornings and thudded through the day. She'd been busy the last two decades preparing meals, shuffling back and forth to soccer practice and dance, quizzing them on their Arabic alphabet before weekend mosque school, running them to the mall. Now her maklooba lasted several days before Samah's husband complained about the odor of fried cauliflower in the fridge. Her neighbor, a white woman who was an administrative assistant at Woodrow Wilson, suggested she apply. Samah's husband was a cardiac surgeon and there were too many hours in the day to fill with just prayer and watching war carnage on Al Jazeera satellite television. They first assigned her to a handicapped girl in a wheelchair. Samah sat beside her in class and opened her textbook and gently placed a pencil in her small curled fist. This year they moved her to SC where the children with severe learning disabilities struggled with basic instruction.

The first week of school, she'd caught Colin staring at her from across the room where the previous aide was speaking softly to him about choices. He was taller than other 6th graders, with curly brown hair and dark blue eyes. He wore khaki pants, not jeans or shorts like the other children.

"Why is she wearing that on her head?" Colin had loudly demanded when he saw Samah.

It didn't break the attention of the five other children who'd given Samah blank looks when she had entered the room that morning. They went back to coloring maps of the United States that Mrs. Werthe, the classroom teacher, had distributed.

"That's not very polite to ask," the aide had said.

Colin's blunt question bothered Samah no more than the staff members who refused to meet her eyes and at least nod hello. They rushed by her, staring down at a stack of papers though she willed them to look up at her when she passed them in the hallway. This child was only being honest. That morning she had walked across the room and said, "Hello. I'm Miss Samah. I wear this—" she'd pointed at her hijab "—because I'm a Muslim and women cover their hair for modesty."

"The 9-11 terrorists were Muslim," Colin had said matter-of-factly.

"Colin!" the aide said. She turned red and had looked at Mrs. Werthe to intervene. Instead, the teacher had leaned over another child and pointed to a worksheet.

Samah was amused. "Yes. They were. But I'm not a terrorist," she told him. "You know, there's good and bad people in the world."

"My mom says there might be a few bad apples in every bunch," Colin said.

Samah smiled. "Your mom's right."

After that day, Colin made a point of coming over to speak with Samah.

"I read Muslims pray on the floor five times a day," Colin reported one morning as soon as he arrived in the classroom. "They face east towards Mecca." He commenced a series of prostrations, holding up his hands parallel to his ears. The other kids observed with fascination. His aide and Mrs. Werthe watched him without smiling.

Samah had laughed. "Very good, Colin. I see you've done your research."

When the other aide quit before Thanksgiving break, Samah was reassigned.

"You seem to have developed a rapport with Colin," Mrs. Werthe said, her lips in a straight line. "It will be an easy transition for him."

That was five months ago though it felt like ages now.

The other boy was staring in the direction of the window. The blinds obscured the row of houses across the street from the school. Samah wondered how many squad cars and ambulances had surrounded the building. She shuddered and fought back tears.

"I'm tired," the other boy said. The room was gray with the lights off, but she could still make out the scuff marks on his sneakers peeking out from his frayed jeans.

"Do you want to lay down?" Samah asked the other boy. She only needed a few seconds to get to the door, past a wall with a "Mind Your Manners" poster and a dry-erase board with the date printed in cobalt blue, past one round table where the children logged their reading minutes and had one-on-one tutoring, past two plastic crates full of soft fidget toys and stress balls. That morning, Colin had been set off by the change in schedule and Samah tried several times to get him to hold the large moon ball that lit up craters wherever you squeezed. Instead, he paced. Now in their corner, he was swaying back and forth on his haunches and he looked like a big bird readying himself for flight.

"I'm tired of everything," the other boy said and the clicking sound stopped. He lifted the gun and held it with both hands, but did not aim it at Samah or Colin. He wasn't really pointing it anywhere, but his hands were steady now. "I'm tired of everyone. These dumb teachers. This fucking shitty school."

Colin's ears perked up at that last obscenity and Samah vigorously nodded her head to him in affirmation that she'd heard it, too, and raised a finger to her lips.

"I get tired, too," Samah told the other boy. "People are not always friendly to me."

"That's because you're a fucking terrorist," the other boy said, but it was almost a whisper like something he'd heard and didn't quite understand.

Colin flinched again and Samah did something without thinking: she placed her hand over his, not holding it, but covering it completely like a second layer of skin. He did not jerk away.

Sixteen years ago, her daughter Maram came home from school, tears streaking her face. A teacher had told her, "your people crashed into the towers." Days later, her son Omar ran from the playground with a bloody nose when the neighborhood kids shoved him off the monkey bars.

"Life will never be the same for us again," Samah's husband had declared. They sat side by side on the couch, watching the footage, the perfect clouds of explosion gradually swallowed by the sky.

Several of her female cousins and girlfriends surrendered the hijab—some of their own accord, others on frightened orders from their husbands. Samah refused to take off the headscarf and succumb to the fear and rage, and there was always a cost to pay for her choice. One afternoon at the supermarket, her young children were in the backseat of her car as she loaded groceries. A can of green peas was thrown at her from across the parking lot and crashed loudly into her car door. Omar and Maram were inconsolable, slapping at the windows, crying and pleading with her to take them home before someone killed them. Another time on her way to her friend Nuha's house, she waited at a stoplight when a middle-aged white man rolled down his car window and spat at her. He pulled behind her, his bumper no longer visible in her rearview mirror because he was so close. He trailed her for several blocks. Fearing he would mark her friend's house, she circled the neighborhood until he finally drove off, laying on the horn as he peeled away. She sat in her friend's driveway, sobbing, before Nuha discovered her through the window and rushed out.

Outside, the rain turned into a thin sheet, coating the roof and windows. The other boy kicked at a chair across from him and it toppled over, startling Samah. She considered how life on this day would change them all again. If she didn't survive, her husband would be a widower. He'd travel alone to hajj next year, a trip they'd planned to take together to Mecca while they were still relatively young. Her children would go on to dance at their weddings and hold up their babies. She would never again stand between them, looping an arm through theirs.

Her cellphone was in her purse in a closet next door. If only she could send a message to her family. She'd tell her husband to eat fruit every day though he already knew this, and she'd tell Omar to watch over his sister and never forget she'll always be an important woman in his life among others, and she'd tell Maram to remember her worth that no man could ever diminish. She'd tell them to be happy, that life was short no matter how old they were.

Samah swallowed a lump of tears. "I'm sure you don't believe I'm a terrorist," she told the other boy. "You've seen me around here and I haven't done anything to hurt you or anyone else. Right?" She held up her hands in a gesture of defenselessness.

The other boy looked up at her with glassy eyes and Samah realized he was crying. From their corner, she could see two narrow streams glistening down the other boy's pale cheeks.

"Don't talk to me!" he shouted, pounding his fist on the table. "I don't care about you! I don't care about any of you!" He began bawling and banged the muzzle of the gun against his forehead. "Why? Why? Why?" he wailed. "I didn't do anything to them. Why?"

Colin unclenched his teeth from the collar of his T-shirt and sat perfectly still. He seemed curious by this outburst. "His forehead's bleeding" he informed Samah.

The other boy smeared the blood away with the back of his hand, regarding it as though he was unsure it was his. Then he looked at them with a strange dullness in his eyes.

Samah sucked her breath in. *Bismallah a rahman a raheem*, she silently prayed, *in the name of God, most merciful and beneficent. Please don't hurt us.* She pressed her hand firmly over Colin's. She could no longer fight her tears.

"Why do they hate me?" the other boy moaned. His forehead looked like someone had dabbed red fingerpaint across it.

Colin sat up. "Who hates you?"

"Jimmy McIntyre, Eddie Lewis, Mike Nolan. I didn't do anything to them."

"I don't know them because I'm in Self-Contained," Colin said.

"Jeannie Wilson plugs her nose when she passes me," the other boy said. "I don't stink."

"My mom says we've been conditioned to dislike our natural body odor," Colin said.

"Shut up! Shut up! Don't talk to me," the other boy snapped.

"Please," Samah said. "He doesn't understand your pain. But I do." Her eyes flitted from his face to the gun.

"I wanna get out of this place," the other boy whined. "I wanna go somewhere nobody will find me."

"You can travel through a wormhole," Colin offered. He folded his legs beneath him and planted his hands in front of him, leaning towards the other boy. "Nobody will ever find you."

He glared at Colin. "What are you even talking about?"

"Wormholes," Colin said. "You could travel to another region of the universe way faster than normal time so if you decided to come back you wouldn't have changed too much."

The other boy was quiet as though he were considering this prospect. He regarded Colin with new interest and slowly walked over to their corner.

Samah pressed Colin's hand. *Master of the Day of Judgment. You alone we worship; You alone we ask for help.* She watched the other boy approach them, gun hanging at his side. It could have been a catcher's mitt, or a toy truck. *Please don't hurt this innocent boy. Please don't hurt me*, she silently prayed.

Up close and standing over them, the other boy was no taller than Colin but he was like a child-giant disturbed from his slumber. Freckles spilled across the bridge of his nose and his eyes were red-rimmed.

"I wouldn't change at all?" he asked Colin. The gun shook at his side.

Colin nodded his head. "It hasn't been completely proven. But scientists say wormholes exist based on the theory of general relativity."

The other boy listened. A shuffle of movement came from outside the classroom door. He turned his head toward it for a second and raised his gun. "Shut up!" he shouted at Colin. "You don't—"

Samah lunged for the gun. There was a crash of sound and a strange pain in her head like she'd been hit with a bat. She felt herself slump back down to her original position in the corner.

The left side of her headscarf was hot and wet. She wanted to raise her fingers and touch the fabric, but she couldn't lift her arm. There was another crash of sound and she watched a blurry mass crumple to the floor near her feet. Colin was shrieking beside her but she couldn't hear it over the ringing in her ears. It felt like a long time before a burst of light flooded the classroom and figures in black vests and faces masked by helmets rushed in and pointed their weapons at the unmoving mass on the floor.

Samah could always tolerate hot summer days outside without breaking a sweat, but the air seemed to be growing thinner in the classroom like it had been lifted to a higher altitude. She wanted desperately to pull off her hijab and tear off her tunic with long sleeves spilling over her wrists, to feel pure, clean air rushing the pores of her face and arms. But she hadn't been bare-skinned in public for over forty years, and she never would again.

Two paramedics carefully positioned her so she lay on her back and one of them—a female, but Samah was not entirely sure—began mouth-to-mouth resuscitation. There was a vague pressure and noises stripped of their treble.

La ilaha illa Allah, Muhammadur rasoolu Allah.

She started to fade away, knowing life would go on and families would tend to their injured and bury their dead in memorials full of flowers and teddy bears, and perhaps a governor would preside.

If those left behind were lucky, their memory might turn into a wormhole and when they came back from the other side, they'd discover everything had changed but them.

PERFECT GENES

I'm wearing a plastic Wonder Woman mask and the matching vinyl costume that kids in the seventies wore over their clothes, with those strings you tied in the back like a hospital gown. My younger brother Mahdi—the Incredible Hulk—is standing next to me, clutching the handle of his Trick O' Treat pumpkin basket, while I hold his free hand. There's a crack in his mask like a jagged scar running down his forehead, and I smile now, holding the photograph and remembering that my mother had sat on it moments before he put it on. We are posed on the porch of a neighbor's bungalow just as she's opening the door, and she's cradling a bowl of candy in the crook of her arm. If you look closely at the photograph you can see a glare from the old woman's cat-eye glasses. My brother and I are bathed in the warm autumn sunlight on Chicago's Southside.

"Found it!" I call from my mother's basement, placing the photograph on the floor beside me. I'm sitting on folded legs and before me is an old Hoover vacuum box that reaches almost four feet in height. It is nearly full to the top with photographs. A combination of mildew and dust permeate the brown marble-colored carpet. I pull out a few Kodak instants stuck together from humidity and peel them apart. I've purchased those pretty storage boxes from Michaels craft store to help my mother organize the photographs. She insists she doesn't have time. Most of our childhood has been similarly neglected: my old Barbies—some naked, some in formal dress attire—are heaped on top of each other in a large, black Hefty bag; Mahdi's *Garbage Patch Kids* collector cards are mixed up with his kindergarten drawings in an old Trapper Keeper that belonged to me in the fourth grade. Report cards are nowhere to be found.

"When do I have time to organize pictures?" my mother demands. "How can I do anything else around here besides cooking and cleaning?"

My mother spent years taking our picture, but no time arranging the snapshots in albums. When we were kids, she drove us to Pixie's drugstore on 55th and California Avenue to develop each roll of film. Mahdi and I took turns holding the small capsule with the coiled film. We would snap the lid off and on with our thumbs until my mother scolded us. Once, Mahdi spied her camera on the kitchen counter and flicked open its back door where you inserted the amber-colored film, exposing it to the light. He didn't realize his mistake until my mother picked up the new batch. Two pictures contained an eerily white blur like a ghost escaping into a wall.

I call to my mother again from the basement. "I found it, Ma!"

"Found what? What are you looking for?" she shouts down from the top of the stairs. Don't make a mess down there, Sabah. She says this part in her colloquial Arabic, and it's half-heartedly strict. Mahdi and I were mostly well-behaved kids. When necessary, my father had been the disciplinarian—a role most Arab mothers would never allow to be usurped. My mother never clamored or fretted over us; she has always been pleasantly detached.

I shift on my knees as nausea sweeps over me. I press my hand against the side of a battered leather sofa and swallow a stream of bile that has swum up my throat. By now, I should have grown accustomed to this nausea, but the specialist insists that side effects of HCG vary from patient to patient. I wonder if the nausea will taste the same when I am finally pregnant, if the bitterness clinging to my teeth that my tongue can't mop away is just as sharp in the first trimester. My hands curl into tight fists and I close my eyes, waiting for it to pass. When I open them, nothing's changed: I'm still on the floor and photographs are scattered around me.

The social committee at the insurance agency where I work is hosting a "Who's That Halloween Baby?" contest and the employee with the most correct guesses wins a Starbucks gift card and one of those obnoxiously enormous containers of candy corn that everyone's been coveting all week, but nobody actually likes to eat.

I'm happy to find a picture that captures a regular American holiday. Shelly, the office manager, will be pleased. "Good morning, Miss Morning," she'll greet me tomorrow as I hand her the photograph. My name Sabah means "morning" and Shelly has been more than amused by this for the five years I have worked at the agency.

I return my haphazardly arranged piles of photographs to the box. I pause to look at some I had only glanced at when I was searching for the Halloween one. A picture slips from a stack and I pick it up.

A blonde and chubby toddler holds the edge of a coffee table and extends her free hand to the camera. She is caught mid-laugh and I can almost hear the gurgling delight in her open mouth. Her blue eyes twinkle. I turn the photograph over. The only inscription is the year—1974—and a solitary, charming name: Layla.

I've never seen this child and yet her face is uncannily familiar. I feel a lump in my chest. I quickly scatter the piles of photographs I had been ready to drop into the Hoover box, and I begin a new search. I need to find one snapshot of me as a baby—two or three years old—to confirm what my heart already knows is true. My hands are frantic and trembling, and I'm clawing at the piles, pulling one then pitching it to one side of the floor.

At last, I find one, then two, and soon three more appear. My nausea rises again, but I don't care. I gather the photographs and flip through them like I'm dealing cards, searching for the best close-up.

Here it is: I'm blithely sitting on my father's lap and my mother is standing behind us at a table laden with themed birthday plates and cups. There's a round cake with a thick numeral one candle, its wick lit and golden-orange. I'm clapping my hands and looking at someone off camera—a relative, I guess—who wants me to mimic their applause. It's our first house in Chicago before we moved to the south suburbs when Mahdi started high school. I recognize a section of paisley curtains that my mother hadn't changed in seventeen years, until my parents put the house up for sale. She bought a solid, hunter-green set to replace the paisley—her only effort to modernize our house.

I take the photograph of the little blonde girl and hold it up to the one of me. It is unmistakable. She's the white version of me. Both of our noses have a small bulb that betrays the adult one I've grown into with a long bridge and narrow nostrils. Our eyes are deeply set and we have prominent foreheads. Not wide and flat, but rounded foreheads that later become the target of cruel jokes like *That's not a forehead—it's a five-head!* I have olive skin and brown eyes; my hair is curly and dark-brown. My mother has left it loose and unfettered in the photograph. These differences are enough to make us complete strangers to undiscerning eyes.

"Ma! Yamma!" I call as I jog up the stairs. My mother is seated at the kitchen table, shaping a mixture of lamb and beef into kufta rolls. She has her silver pan ready—aged with grease stains and happy dents—and arranges the meat, filling in spaces with potato wedges and chopped onions. When it is nearly baked, she adds sliced tomatoes and their juices sizzle at the bottom of the hot pan.

"Habibti, turn off the stove before my rice burns," she instructs me.

I can feel her gaze on my back, but when I turn around, she pretends to be looking over my shoulder at some invisible object floating there. I know she's worried about me, but I've told her repeatedly that these things sometimes take time, that Nader and I are seeing one of the best specialists in Illinois. She tries hard to be kind about my gradual weight gain from the hormones.

"Are you still walking every day?" she casually asks.

"Yes, of course," I say curtly. "Yama, who is this?" I hold the photograph in front of her face. My mother reaches for it and remembers her fingers are covered in the soft, whitish fat of the meat.

"Oh. Bint abooki—that's your father's daughter," she says matter-of-factly.

This has always been my mother's way: no excitement, no need for getting worked up. There's no change in her tone, no elevation in the tempo of her statement. She may have said, *Oh. That's your father's old coat or Oh. That's your father's favorite tie.*

"You've seen it, mish ah?" She continues arranging the ingredients in the pan, her eyes impervious to the raw onions.

"What are you talking about, Yamma! "I say incredulously. "Baba's daughter? How? When?"

My mother pauses and rubs her forehead against her shoulder, careful of the grease still on her hands. "I'm sure you knew."

The photograph becomes an extension of my hand as I wave it, appalled, attempting to extract a reasonable explanation from my mother. A dull pain throbs in my hip, but I ignore it and concentrate on the picture.

"Yamma. I have never seen it—her—before." As soon as I refer to the toddler out loud, she becomes three-dimensional like someone who has just entered the kitchen, interrupting the conversation I'm having with my mother. On any other afternoon our discussion would be laced with questions regarding my treatments. Lately, nothing has been more urgent in our lives. Until now. I look at the toddler in the photograph, where precise corners seal the entire scene. Inside of it she's oblivious, unscathed.

"It was before your father married me," she says, hoping this reassures me and absolves my father of any guilt. "I insisted he send for her. I told him I would raise her—wallah, I did."

"What happened?" I ask. My voice is like the echo of an unfamiliar sound, already fading.

"Your father refused. He claimed she wasn't his, but I knew better. Your uncle's wife, Widad, told me all about that white woman." She smirks. "Widad couldn't wait to tell me the details—that spiteful cow." With her elbows, my mother pushes her chair back from the table and washes her hands. She covers the pan with shiny aluminum foil and sets it in the fridge. She'll cook it an hour before my father comes home so that it is steaming hot the way he likes it.

I need to sit down. "Why didn't he keep in touch with her?" I ask, settling in a chair while my mother wipes the table down.

"Like I said—he convinced himself that she wasn't his. He told me the marriage had been for his citizenship. Your grandfather, Seedo Ismail, compensated the woman. But, I'm fairly certain Seedo never knew about the baby; it would have broken his heart." She rinses the dishcloth and reaches for the coffee pot on the granite counter. "I need some qahwa. Would you like a cup?"

I ignore her questions and any superfluous statements my mother uses to cloak this discovery. She has no part in my father's secret past, but I feel she is complicit. Just like the pile of photographs—disorganized, scattered—my mother uncannily leaves things alone. Her home is clean, but unkempt. Laundry is washed daily and yet it remains unfolded for days or until I grab a hamper of dried towels and my father's woolen socks, folding them while she cooks.

"I can't believe it, Ma. How could he do that? How could you let him abandon her?"

My mother is startled by these questions, and for the first time she sees my dismay. "Why are you upset, habibti? Between you and me, she was better off without Baba. Your father was not an easy man when he first came to this country. He seemed to have forgotten his religion and did haram. Drinking, gambling. Elhamdulillah he straightened up before I met him." She sits again at the table and examines her fingernails. She scoops bits of meat out of them with her longest pinky nail.

The cordless phone rings near my elbow on the table and I pick it up. It's my father calling from his store. "Hi, Baba," I say, my voice shaky. I grip the phone tightly to steady my trembling hand. My mother stops picking at her fingernails and watches me.

"Baba," I begin.

He sounds tired on the other end. "How are you, habibti?"

"I'm fine." I hand my mother the phone.

* * *

That night, Nader leans over and offers my cheek a tender kiss. We have just made love and sink back into a heap of pillows. We have been making love the same way for the last year: we are tender with each other, but an urgency of purpose beyond love and desire invades our sheets. We're like lost and starving interlopers invading someone's private campsite and pillaging their food. This need to produce a baby pounds away at our limbs and we bite down hard on our lips until we're raw, inside and out. Afterwards, we're exhausted and try hard not to look into each other's eyes for too long.

Nader folds me into his arms, breathing hard and hot against the crown of my head. I smell his sweat and spicy aftershave as my face rests against his chest. His hand grabs my hip and I wince. Every night I stand astride him as he sits on our bed, nervously preparing the needle that swishes with alien hormones prepared to vanquish my own weak ones. He asks me several times if I'm ready before he plunges it deep into my flesh. I know he's disgusted for a few moments and works hard to flush out the revulsion from his brain before he holds my face up for a kiss, his hand automatically cupping my breast.

The first time Nader had to administer the needle he couldn't get an erection. I felt hollow and lonely, imagining my trapped egg, mature and ready, waiting inside its follicle. But, we soon discovered the follicle is devious; it cruelly nourishes my egg, but won't let it go.

If the ovum is not released, a corpus luteum does not develop, the doctor told us in his gray-carpeted and gray-wallpapered office. He touched his iPad and we silently watched a graphic animation of ovulation failure. A ten year old could understand my deficiency.

I wait until Nader has fallen asleep, until his soft snoring is a rhythmic pattern. I slip out of bed and quietly trot down the staircase, the framed photographs of our wedding spiraling down the wall. At the bottom, a handsomely carved table holds a crystal vase with fresh white carnations and a ceramic mail sorter I painted. Anna, the middle-aged Polish housekeeper I hire once a month, cleaned today and I can see the glint of wood polish bounce off the table as the moonlight filters through the bay window of the foyer. I find my purse in the coat closet and pull out the picture.

I sink onto the sofa in the living room, against velvet pillows that Anna fluffed and replaced in an orderly line. The room smells of Febreeze and vanilla-scented candles. I hold the photograph a few inches from my face. I worry that Nader will wake up so I don't turn on the lamp, but gaze fixedly on the image that I know now by heart. Every detail is vivid in my mind's eye from her red-and-green jumper and white knit turtleneck, to her cobalt eyes. She's wearing those old-fashioned saddle shoes. Her sparse strawberry-blonde hair is pulled into a pigtail on top of her head. Mahdi and I certainly had more hair at that age according to the few pictures my mother has actually framed and still displays atop her dresser.

Layla. I think about the advantages of such a name, all the interesting possibilities.

Does she tell people it's Eric Clapton's "Layla," or does she make up a story about my father, a man she has no memory of except maybe when she dreams?

Here's the story I prefer to imagine: Thirty years ago, her mother—maybe a waitress in some 24-hour diner—serves a strange, but handsome Middle Eastern man. He leaves her a generous tip and returns every night for a week until he wears down her resolve. *One night was all it took*, Layla tells her friends, *and here I am.*

I want to know if she worries like me and if she laughs with a snort like Mahdi. I wonder if she was popular in school or terribly shy. Did she love science, but dreaded gym as I did? Is she a Christian, and maybe reads a little about Islam because she's curious—or did she lose someone in 9/11 over a decade ago and thinks she'll find answers in a book a white man has written?

There's Palestinian in her, perhaps in the way she might feel hopeless one moment then irrationally optimistic the next. Does she know it? Or, maybe she gladly denies it because so little proof remains.

I wonder if she's married. With children. Or, do her eggs shrivel up like mine?

I trace the circumference of her head with my pinky finger.

No, no.

I'm convinced she has inherited the best from our father, his strong and robust reproductive genes, thriving like sunflowers. That would be her perfect retribution—*bakht,* as my mother calls it—for being denied by our father.

In the dark, Layla's image is shadowy except for the small hand she extends to the camera. I'm certain it's my father taking the picture, which he'll later deny when I finally ask him. I hear him cooing her name until she looks up and he snaps the shutter. *Layla, habibti,* he says.

Does she even know that *Layla* means *night*—that by nature, she and I are two polar creatures?

There on the sofa in my desperately noiseless house, I whisper in the darkness, *Layla and Sabah.* We are night and day.

Snake Eyes

Mahmoud stared at his wife's gold bangles—her asawar—sitting in the deposit space after the owner of the pawnshop pushed them back through the window. The glass opening was just wide enough for a pair of baby shoes or an electric shaver. Enough space to shove your hand through and wiggle your fingers at the owner. He'd take your item, call his price, and then push it back to you. It was like limbo. The transactional item—a baseball signed by Hank Aaron that was once perched on someone's mantle, or a folding spear-blade knife safely returned from Iraq—sat awaiting its judgment.

"Three hundred—tops," the owner told Mahmoud. He always punctuated his appraisal with *tops* though nearly every item was negotiable. If Mahmoud managed to squeeze another fifty dollars out of the deal, the man would briskly say, "Okay. One-fifty. Tops." He wore a pinstriped bowling shirt with a sewn-in nametag that wasn't his name. He was tall and spindly with a pockmarked face, and he looked like he'd seen it all from behind the plated glass window and was prepared to handle any bullshit. His tired eyes never left Mahmoud's face.

The red and yellow disks of a traffic light on Larkin Avenue reflected in the security mirror above the entrance of the pawnshop. Cars slowed to a stop then screeched away, their stereo bass unnerving to Mahmoud. The Empress Casino was only two miles away.

"Three-hundred," Mahmoud repeated. It seemed as inevitable a conclusion as having to fix a flat tire. "I'll take it."

As the owner swiftly tagged the bangles, Mahmoud vowed he wouldn't hock any more of his wife's jewelry. He knew if he came back later he was likely to see his wife's asawar illuminated by a track of florescent light bulbs inside the glass display case. Hayfa had worn them last month at her nephew's wedding reception and they'd jangled with each excited clap of her hands during the young couple's first dance. She'd squeezed his thigh beneath the round dining table, smiling at him with lower teeth.

"Thanks, man," Mahmoud said. He folded the bills three times and stowed them in the front pocket of his pants.

"Good luck," the shop owner said, returning to his newspaper.

Mahmoud walked quickly to his car parked on a residential side street outside the pawnshop. A few of the houses were burnt out. In the windows of others, twisted vinyl blinds dangled or the frames had been completely boarded up. Sitting on the stoop of one house, a small group of black men smoked cigarettes in the brisk October night. Their laughter echoed close to Mahmoud and for a moment he wanted to join them, to forget about winning and losing, and to feel their easy mirth rise up from his own belly.

He turned his keys in the ignition and looked at his reflection in the visor mirror. He had bags under his eyes that worried Hayfa. He ran his fingers through his receding hair, once thick and wavy and full of spicy-smelling product. Nowadays he had the barber trim it as close to his scalp as possible. Hayfa complained he looked like a refugee from the mokhayam where she was born—before he brought her to the States. He turned fifty-two yesterday and each year seemed to creak in his bones when he moved. Fifty had produced a vague melancholy he'd thought natural for a man steeped in middle age. But, something precipitated by the physical decline of his body had begun to rattle him and he felt a terrible dread deep in his bones. While he witnessed his daughters growing into themselves, their slender and strong legs extending from sturdy torsos, he noticed more wrinkles around Hayfa's eyes that had not been there before and that it took him slightly more heft to climb out of bed or pull upright from off the toilet seat. He'd been aging for a decade, but had only recently acknowledged the changes. Another decade would pass and unlike his daughters— they would thrive from their education, make money independent of him, and in careers of their choosing, and fall in love multiple times without a contingency of marriage—it felt like an ominous end, the distance closing between him and a trap wall.

Mahmoud flicked up the visor and pulled away, the shedding branches of trees casting shadows like bony arms and fingers across his dashboard. It was almost midnight. His daughters would be on the verge of sleep, their teenage frenetic bodies finally succumbing to the exhaustion of algebra and volleyball practice. They would forget to pull out their iPod ear buds and turn off the television set mounted on each of their bedroom walls. Hayfa would check in on them, picking up dirty ankle socks off the beige carpeted floor. She would soundlessly flick switches, close computer screens and gather empty Gatorade bottles. Before she lay down in their bed, she would rub some Nivea cream up and down her arms and in small circles around her elbows.

As he stepped out of the parking tower and into the casino lobby, Mahmoud left any thoughts of his wife and their children sealed in the elevator.

* * *

He became indifferent to the casino's shoddy brownish-red brick exterior like all the depressed buildings in Joliet. The courthouse was just a few blocks away, and the adult detention center Mahmoud had initially found disconcerting to be so close, sat impassively across the street. There was broken pavement along the perimeter of the half-mile block it sat on and garbage was strewn near gutters and within a vacant lot behind it.

Inside, red and black diamonds carpeted one end of the casino to a grand buffet restaurant on the other end. People milled around the player tables or sat in front of slot machines with hands poised on the old-fashioned levers.

The first time he released the dice Mahmoud felt his muscles constrict in his chest. It wasn't a vigorous roll; the dice did not sail across the green and spring off the back of the table. He was nervous and clumsy, grateful at least the dice hadn't skipped onto the floor. He'd done what someone else at the table did: he laid each die with the desirable sum of the numbers face-up.

Inshallah, he prayed then immediately winced at his own blasphemy.

"Seven out," the dealer announced, sweeping his dice stick across the table.

It was a whirlwind. Before Mahmoud could blink, his stack of chips was swept away from him and other shooters were already laying down their next bets.

Every sound in the casino seemed at once distinct and blended: the *click, click, click* of a roulette ball, making its final passage into a slot; the trilling of slot machines as coins happily dispensed into a steel tray, a player waiting to scoop them up; the clinking of half-empty glasses abandoned on the edges of tables, gathered up in twos by the deft fingers of weary waitresses with smoker's rings under their eyes and thinning hair teased and pulled up in a French twist. Mahmoud's body absorbed all these noises when he lost and his muscles tingled and tightened under his skin. He breathed deeply through is nose before getting to his feet, to "shake it off" as Ted, one of the dealers, suggested.

At first, he was just another anonymous gambler—another crystallized player at the craps table. If he recognized arrabi acquaintances, he avoided catching their eyes and hoped they'd just move along. The times they acknowledged him, he'd lie and say with mock exasperation that he lost his brother-in-law somewhere around the casino.

Tonight, Mahmoud arrived and played through the start of Ted's shift. A box-man stood a few feet away from the craps table, obstinate and watching.

"Hey there, Mac," Ted greeted Mahmoud. "How they hangin'?"

Ted was in his late forties with a strong medium build. His long-sleeve uniform did little to conceal powerful arms, and his muscles strained against the fabric when he gathered chips. His sandy-blonde hair was parted down the middle and feathered like he was still living in the 1980s. He had kind blue eyes, almost disappearing when he smiled. Mahmoud was happy to see him.

Something about Ted relaxed him and he could forget about Hayfa's golden bangles in a glass display smudged with fingerprints. But when he was down five-hundred bucks in less than an hour, Mahmoud slunk lower on his stool at the edge of the table, and not even Ted could bolster him. He felt his bowels loosen. He pressed his palm against the front of his pants where the remaining hundred dollar bills were momentarily safe.

By three a.m., he'd lost most of it. He left Ted and the table to sit at the bar for a while.

That's when he saw her for the first time.

She was wearing a tight short cocktail dress and flashed a swath of her white panties when she hoisted herself onto a barstool. She looked no more than fifteen like his daughter Raya whom he'd started teaching to drive in the Costco parking lot on early Sunday mornings. But, this white girl had on too much make-up and carried a clutch purse, which she lightly tapped against the bar as she waited for her drink. She sat close to a much older man who had his hand on her thigh. They laughed and she playfully poked his arm.

Mahmoud watched her, his stomach cramping. He had the sensation of diarrhea and nausea all at once, but sat still, knowing it would pass as soon as he settled himself on the bar stool. He'd lost the three-hundred Hayfa's bangles had yielded, and some of the money he'd set aside to pay Jameel who managed his mobile phone store. A third warning was always sent before his store lost electricity, phone and water. He'd manage to win enough to cover his work expenses. Only once was the water supply shut off. He and Jameel had to piss in the alley for two days until a utility man restored it so they were able to flush the toilet in the back of the store.

The white girl was now leaning into the older man and whispering something in his ear. Suddenly, the man jerked back his liver-spotted hand as though her thigh was on fire and waved her away, shaking his head. She brushed off the rejection and moved to the center of the bar.

Mahmoud hoped she wouldn't solicit him.

"Hi," she said.

Up close, he saw a cluster of white heads on her chin, poorly concealed by creamy make-up. Her blonde highlights had receded to the middle of her head, just above her ears, and it made her naturally brown hair look like a sheet of wet sand. Her lips were plump and fleshy like she was constantly chewing them.

"I'm not interested," Mahmoud said quickly. He felt foolish and a little afraid.

"I'm not either, Babu," she said, rolling her gray eyes.

"You're a very rude young lady," he said, his embarrassment fading to annoyance.

"Hey. I was just being polite when you insulted me like I was a hooker or something," she huffily declared.

He could see one of her incisor teeth was missing, and a silver ball in the center of her tongue repugnantly bounced up and down in her mouth when she spoke.

He was quiet for a few moments. "You're right. I apologize," he told her. "Good night." The last thing he wanted was to make a scene with the young woman.

"Thank you," she said. She swiveled from side to side on her barstool, watching him leave. "Hey, Mister. Could you buy me dinner at the buffet? I wasn't so lucky at black jack tonight."

He turned back to her. It was three a.m. Hayfa was already asleep. Inside the casino, the absence of natural light made it easy to linger. You couldn't tell if the sun had set—or risen, for that matter.

"Or breakfast," she added when Mahmoud looked at his watch.

He cleared his throat and considered her request. Without the heavy make-up and skimpy dress, she could have been a member of his daughters' volleyball team, or maybe a friend in their study group for final exams, or a partner on a class project, who'd call her parents to let them know she'd eaten after Hayfa insisted she try her stewed okra with lamb chunks.

Mahmoud finally nodded and moments later the white girl plopped down across from him in a booth with two full plates of food. She scooped mashed potatoes into her mouth, talking while she ate—a quality that made her seem even younger.

"Sorry," she said. I haven't eaten in forever.

Mahmoud sipped a bitter cup of coffee. "What are you doing here?"

She wiped her mouth with a paper napkin, chomped on a drumstick then wiped her mouth again before answering. "Trying to get lucky," she said. "Aren't you going to eat anything? This is the 'Epic Buffet' after all."

"No, no. I'm fine," he said.

"Not even dessert? They have the best almond cookies in this place." She picked up her sloppily arranged taco and crunched until its shell cracked down the middle. "Shit," she said. She scooped up the mixture of greasy ground beef, shredded lettuce and diced tomatoes with her fork. "At least try their cookies."

Mahmoud shook his head. She was smaller sitting across from him in the booth than at the bar. He noticed her thin pale wrists had fresh scabs and faded scratches. When she caught him looking, she put her fork down and placed both hands in her lap.

"So what are you doin' here all by yourself?" she asked.

"Losing," Mahmoud said. He pushed his cup and saucer away from him and folded his arms on the table. "How old are you?"

She left one hand in her lap and tentatively picked up her fork again. "Twenty-two." She looked over her shoulder at the dessert case and jumped up. "I'm going to get you an almond cookie. I promise, one bite and you'll be hooked."

Mahmoud watched her as she scrutinized the green Jell-O cubes and rotated a plate of strawberry-topped cheesecake. She turned back to Mahmoud with a scrunched up nose and stuck out her tongue. With plastic tongs, she picked up three cookies and set a small plate of them in front of Mahmoud. She smiled triumphantly after he took a bite and nodded in satisfaction.

"I told you so!" she said. "They're as good as the ones in Chinatown, right?"

"What's your name?" he asked. It was a dangerous question. He thought of Hayfa.

"Tyler."

"Tyler," Mahmoud repeated. "Isn't that a boy's name?"

"Unisex," she said, nibbling on an asparagus spear. She pointed it at him. "What's yours?"

"Mac."

"That's not your real name," she said. "Tell me your real name." She chewed to the middle of the stalk then dropped it on her plate. She ate the rest of the asparagus this way.

"Muh-mood," he said, slowly and loudly enunciating it as though speaking to a deaf person.

"Mu-mood," Tyler repeated.

"You can just call me Mac." Before he could catch himself, he asked her, "Do you need a ride home?"

"No thanks."

"I can drive you," Mahmoud said. He imagined her automatically clicking on her seatbelt, looking into the visor mirror the way his daughter Rania did to touch her face and fluff her hair before he'd drop her and Raya off at the mall on a Saturday afternoon. Before he'd bought Rania her first car and she no longer needed him.

"Look, mister. I appreciate the meal," she said. She broke a cookie in half. "I'm hanging out for a while." Her gray eyes darted around the restaurant, avoiding his.

Less than an hour ago he had hoped she wouldn't look his way. Now he was offering her a ride home. She was young and disarming. Hayfa would have seen that too, and understood the situation.

Ya haram, she might have said. *What a shame!*

She ate the rest of the cookie and grabbed her purse. "Thanks for the meal." She slid out of the booth and quickly walked away.

The hostess's disapproving frown swiftly turned into a smile for Mahmoud as he walked out of the Epic Buffet.

* * *

Both he and Hayfa had a safe deposit key for the lockbox at the bank. Hayfa rarely wore the heavier pieces like her kalada—the most popular among fellahin like his family. The last time she had worn the multi-coin necklace was at their engagement party, when he had dressed her with every piece he had purchased with his mother's guidance. By the end of the ceremony, Hayfa looked like she might tip over from the weight of the yellow gold. She was youthful in her pale blue satin dress with the puffed-up lace shoulders. Her expression was a happy one—a dowry of ten thousand dollars in twenty-four carat gold had sealed her future. Back in 1989, that was more than a respectable amount. For a girl from a refugee camp, it was like hitting the lottery.

Mahmoud had exchanged the more expensive pieces at Cash 4 Gold where he knew he'd get the better rate than at a pawnshop. Over ten months of gambling, Mahmoud cleaned out his wife's trousseau. He began rummaging in her jewelry chest in their spacious walk-in closet for miscellaneous pieces amounting to a few thousand dollars. The golden bangles were the first he'd stolen out of their home. He was surprised how easy it was.

***

Mahmoud didn't see Tyler again at the Empress. Weeks passed and he stopped looking for her.

Hayfa had been worried about his general unease and displeasure, pressing him to confide in her what was wrong. He brushed her off, hoping she'd retreat into their daughters' lives and her own world of arabiyat whose husbands worked into retirement so their wives could drive the latest M-series. Lately, he couldn't get an erection, but she dismissed this as a symptom of age and fatigue. And Hayfa did not complain.

One night, he'd brought enough cash to last him till early morning, but he'd still taken a bracelet, tucked away in his sports coat pocket. Just in case. It was one of the few pieces Hayfa actually kept in the house, stored safely in a black velvet case in her jewelry chest. He had left the empty case under the seat of his car when he took the bracelet tonight.

At midnight, someone tapped his shoulder at the craps table. It was Tyler.

Her hair was dyed a rich mahogany making her grayish eyes greener than what he remembered. She wore a spandex miniskirt that reached just below her buttocks and a sheer tank top and lacy bra. Her breasts were small and pushed up high. She looked like a young girl playing dress-up.

"Hello, Mu-mood!" she said, tapping his shoulder again.

"Tyler. Hello," he said, turning back to the table. Their knowing each other deeply embarrassed him. He looked at Ted who gave him a dry smile. It was not unkind, but like the pawnshop owner, the dealer looked at him with no surprise.

"Can I talk to you for a sec?" Tyler asked. She kept her hand on his shoulder, breathing into his ear. She smelled like green apples and sweat.

"I'm in the middle of a game," Mahmoud said, refusing to face her. His cheeks flushed with shame.

"Just for one second, dude!" she said. "C'mon." She squeezed his arm.

"Have a good night, Mac," Ted said, already smiling at a woman who took Mahmoud's spot.

Tyler sidled up to him as they moved through the Friday night crowd. A bachelorette party had arrived with a bride wearing a pink satin sash and plastic tiara, stumbling between the slot machines, maudlin and drunk. Her yawning and barefoot bridesmaids trailed behind her, their strappy heels dangling from their fingers and their mascara running in tiny pools under their eyes like smudges on the faces of football players.

Tyler knocked against his back as she stumbled behind him through the crowd. "Are you hungry, Mu-mood?" Tyler asked over his shoulder.

There was a line at the Epic Buffet. People were talking loud as they waited, some gesturing with drink glasses they brought from the bar. A younger group was celebrating a birthday. They huddled together while someone held up a digital camera high in the air and clicked. The successive and rapid flashes distracted Tyler as Mahmoud tried to talk to her.

"What's going on, Tyler?" Mahmoud asked. She wasn't paying attention to him, instead listening to the banter of the birthday group and laughing along as though she were a member. They politely ignored her.

"Tyler?"

"What? What?" She swung her head towards him as though it were connected to her neck by a pivot. Her eyes were glassy and her pupils dilated. She was high.

"You need some coffee."

She grabbed the flaps of his sports jacket. "I'm hungry," she said, the silver ball bobbing on her tongue. Her sour breath made his nostrils bristle.

"I think you need to sober up," Mahmoud said.

He prepaid for their meals and they were seated at a booth. Mahmoud ordered coffee for both of them while Tyler scooted off the seat to get some food. She walked unsteadily from one buffet station to the next, patting her empty plate against her thigh as she peered over vats of crusty meals. A few patrons balancing bowls of soup or loaded plates noticed her and moved out of her way so she wouldn't knock into them. When she returned, macaroni and cheese was the only thing on her plate.

"Drink some water," Mahmoud said, placing a perspiring glass in front of her. He tore open a straw and popped it in as he had done for his children at restaurants when they were younger. He wondered now if they had ever gotten high, or if they'd taken a sip of beer with their white friends. They mostly stayed in arrabi circles where they'd forged bonds with girls from the Islamic school they attended on Sundays when they were little. Were there girls like Tyler they'd avoided and whispered about in their classes? What would they say if they saw their father in a booth with this young woman? Mahmoud shifted uncomfortably, perspiration seeping into his shirt collar. He felt a sudden trepidation like when he knew the numbers wouldn't come as soon as he released the dice.

"So what's new, Mu-mood?" She took small bites and chewed for a long time.

He was glad they had the privacy of a booth. The line of patrons dwindled and the noise inside the restaurant fell. He saw one of the servers from the casino, a short blonde with thick calves, chatting with the hostess. She had on a Chicago Bears zipped-up hoodie over her uniform. It was an incongruous, almost jarring look, like the time Mahmoud and Hayfa took their children to Disney World and spotted a Cinderella running in Nike sneakers to her post. It somehow broke a spell.

He looked at Tyler. Her hairline was beaded with sweat and her liquid eyes gradually became lucid.

"My mother's a bitch," she said matter-of-factly, tugging at her multi-studded earlobe. "Cares more about her boyfriend, who's totally gay, by the way, and just using her for money." She tore off the paper napkin ring and let her silverware fall onto the table with a clank.

"He'll only let her blow him. They never actually fuck. Don't you think that's, like, a red flag right there?" She mashed the noodles until they blended with the cheese then pushed the plate away.

This was the problem with amarkan, Mahmoud thought. Hayfa would never put anything or anyone before their daughters.

"Anyway, she kicked me out," Tyler said. She drummed black acrylic nails against her glass of water.

"Do you have a job?" Mahmoud gently pushed her cup of coffee closer to her arm.

"Yeah. I mean no. Not yet." She scratched one of her wrists. "I applied for this position at Dave and Busters. You know, dumping all those winning tickets in a plastic tub and weighing them so kids can get a prize. I think I got it. They're supposed to call me back in a few days."

"How are you getting home?"

"I came with someone. He's still playing." She scooted closer to him and let her hand drop in his lap. She rested her head against his shoulder. Flakes of dandruff crusted down the long part in her hair.

"Tyler," he said. His groin stirred, an unpleasant sensation prickling the skin like needles.

"Shhh…" She pinched his lips closed into a duck's bill and began to awkwardly rub his crotch.

Mahmoud peeled her fingers away from his mouth and grabbed her wrist under the table. His face was hot.

"C'mon, dude," she said. "You look like you could use a pick-me-up." She laughed tiredly, her eyelids half-open. Freeing her wrist from his grasp, she attempted to cup his flaccid penis.

"What's this?" She grazed the snake bracelet in his coat pocket when Mahmoud pulled her hand away again. It seemed wrong to let her touch anything belonging to his wife.

"I need to use the restroom," he said and walked quickly away from the booth.

The porcelain tile gleamed against his shoes as he urinated. A man came out of a stall, his face sagging with a familiar loss. He did not bother to wash his hands. At the sink, Mahmoud peered at his reflection in the mirror. The overhead lights cast an image that was his own face, but more stringent, more electrified. His unshaven cheeks were thin and sallow, white hairs penetrating black stubble.

He splashed cool water on his face and accepted a paper towel from the restroom attendant, an old black man sitting on a chair at the end of a long vanity, nodding and smiling good-naturedly at him. Mahmoud pulled his wallet out of his back pocket and gave the old man a five-dollar bill.

Before leaving the restroom, he felt inside his sports coat pocket for the bracelet. He pulled it out and turned the coiled snake so that its golden head was facing him, its ruby eyes entrancing more than menacing.

Mahmoud's mother had insisted on it when they were shopping for Hayfa's muhir.

El hayya! his mother exclaimed. *She must have at least one, habibi.*

At this memory, bile shot up his throat and his legs became unsteady. He wasn't sure he could walk without collapsing.

"You alright, sir?" the old man asked him.

Mahmoud pressed a trembling hand against the wall and laid the other on his hip, keeping his head down until the nausea passed.

He wondered how long it would take to replace the gold he had stolen from Hayfa, knowing it would be less time than it would be for her to forgive him. He'd make it up to her every day from now on.

Maybe they could go to the Dells for a weekend—she always loved it there. When the girls were younger, he'd spend time chasing them around the waterpark while Hayfa shopped at the novelty stores for Wisconsin cheese and jams, and those feathery dream-catchers she'd hang over her rearview mirror. Most of the attractions would be closed for the season, but he and Hayfa could stroll the main street, her arm hooked through his. They always walked like this, his hands tucked deep inside the pockets of his jeans, and she keeping stride, pointing at shop windows, caressing his arm.

Mahmoud stepped out of the restroom and stood in the lobby where the spectacle of flashing lights and noises from the casino floor barely reached him over the thudding of his heart in his ears. His body suddenly swelled with hope, the kind that was both wonderful and terrifying because he knew he didn't deserve it. He rushed past the Epic Buffet where Tyler still sat in a booth, eating chocolate pudding from a cup, oblivious to the world around her and trusting he would come back, which was always a gamble.

WINGSPAN

As they neared Sodus Township, Jasir noticed more American flags suspended over screen doors and others flapping on front yard poles against the brisk autumn winds. He saw one bumper sticker on the back of a pick-up truck that read, IF YOU WANT TO BURN OUR FLAG, WRAP YOURSELF IN IT FIRST.

"You think I'll be safe out here in the backwoods?" he joked with Brian.

"Don't worry, "Brian said. "You'll blend right in."

Jasir pulled off his Chicago Bears cap, ran his fingers through his mashed down thick black hair, and replaced the cap. He looked at his fingernails, cleanly clipped except for a hangnail he'd been teasing which had turned the skin around it red and tender. He chewed it off.

Jasir had been to Michigan plenty of times with Ruba, but they had always driven right through Benton Harbor and straight to Dearborn to eat at Lebanese restaurants that lined every broken, concrete block. He purchased Um Kalthum and Fairuz music CDs for his mother on the way home.

They drove down a narrow gravel road, winding to a ranch house. It had a low-slung porch in the front and dark green shutters. Jasir could see the silhouettes of a few cats slumbering under the porch. A silo loomed behind a red-roofed barn. It reminded him of a poem he'd once read in grammar school.

Brian's uncle took one step at a time off the porch when they approached. He was tall and heavy, shoulders stooped forward as though he were carrying a load on his back. He was clear-eyed with ruddy cheeks, and a few broken capillaries branching out from around his nose gave him a friendly look.

"This is Jasir," Brian said after giving his uncle a hearty embrace. "This is Uncle Lloyd."

"Good to meet you, Jason," Lloyd said.

Jasir did not bother to correct the older man. He vigorously shook his hand, not wanting to disappoint. "Thanks for having me."

"You been hunting before, Jason?"

"No, sir," Jasir said. "Looking forward to it."

A petite woman appeared in the doorway, tidy in a knit sweater and jeans. Two graying plaits of hair looped around her head, fastened by old-fashioned tortoise combs.

"Brian, sweetie! You too old to give Auntie a kiss?"

Brian leaped up the porch steps and lifted the woman, swinging her around a few times until she playfully pounded his chest.

"This is my friend Jasir," Brian told her, waving him over.

"Welcome—Jay-sir, is it?" She shook his hand and continued to hold it, leading him inside. "You boys hungry?"

She opened the door wide and stood aside.

Jasir nudged Brian who pointed down a hallway to a bathroom. The wallpaper was navy-blue and the seams were coming undone along the edges where it met the wooden floor panels. It held a pattern of old-fashioned anchors and ship wheels. Ruba would have called it quaint—like the quaintness of a bed-and-breakfast where they had spent a weekend in Galena. They had held hands when walking through novelty shops and boutiques, and she had turned to him every time to test an aroma of homemade candles or the softness of fleece blanket. That was the last weekend they had tried very hard together.

On a small shelf was a row of extra toilet paper; each roll was dressed in a crocheted cover. There was a bar of lemon-grass hand soap instead of a pump, and after lathering, Jasir rinsed it clear of suds before replacing it on the dish.

He removed his cap and raked his hair so it regained its volume. His olive skin appeared darker in the soft light cast above the vanity. He massaged the stubble on his chin and examined his profile. He had decided to grow a beard—or maybe a goatee. He picked up a tube of L'Occitane, which he figured belonged to Lloyd's wife, and wondered if Ruba had finished packing her stuff. She had already cleared the bathroom of her expensive salon products—massive one-liter pumps of shampoo and conditioner—and removed her terrycloth robe from the hook behind the door.

At the dinner table, the only thing Jasir could eat that was halal was the sweet potato casserole Brian's aunt beamed over as she served. He tried to avoid looking at the peppered pork roast with glazed vegetables sitting in the middle of dining table. It irked him that Brian had forgotten his restricted diet, but still he hoped nobody would notice he wasn't eating much.

Lloyd chewed while he talked. "What are you—Greek?" he asked Jasir. "Like that Jason and the Argo-Nuts?" He smiled widely then resumed chewing.

"He's from Palestine," Brian interjected. It sounded like the ancient, biblical place that it was when amarkan said it.

"You mean near Bethlehem?" his aunt asked. She had kept her apron on at the table and continuously refilled everyone's glasses and scooped multiple helpings onto their plates. "Where Jesus was born?"

Jasir smiled and nodded, chewing a homemade biscuit that left his mouth dry and starchy. "My parents were born less than ten miles from Bethlehem." This was what he usually told people so they would feel momentarily less awkward about his identity.

"Is that a fact?" Lloyd said, his head cocked to one side as he examined Jasir in a newly interested way. "That's where all them Jews and Ay-rabs are still fighting over the land."

Brian's aunt suddenly looked confused as though she wasn't sure which was more unsettling—a Jew or an Arab sitting at her table. But her Christian manners never faltered and she insisted Jasir have a third helping of the sweet potato casserole.

* * *

They played beanbags after dinner in the open yard until their breaths became visible puffs of air. Autumn had brushed through the surrounding landscape in sweeping magnificence, in the last of the defiant dandelions, their stems and leaves starting to curl towards the earth; through the red maple trees on either side of Lloyd's house, their leaves a brilliant and feverish scarlet, and the sugar maples with still-orange leaves, their bark shaggy and rough. There were large terra cotta planters brimming with pale pink and deep purple chrysanthemums.

Jasir concentrated hard on the glazed wooden panel, raised like a platform he might have jumped off with his skateboard when he was a kid. He held his beanbag in front of him, slightly below his chest, pumping it in his palm before loosening it to the air. His trajectory fell short every time, missing the hole in the wooden panel by several feet. Sometimes he'd miss the entire panel, his beanbag landing on the cold grass with a defeated thump. At one point, he managed to knock out his opponent's bag, but that was all. Lloyd, stout like an oak tree, stood behind the wooden panel, reclining on the heels of his work boots, fingers and thumbs hooked into the loops of jeans.

After Jasir's last failed toss, Lloyd shook his head and chuckled. "Shooting oughta be in-er-esting tomorrow," he said.

When Brian's uncle and aunt retired to bed, Brian led Jasir to the barn and they shared a joint while talking about the doctors and nurses at the hospital where they worked as IT reps, training staff to use their iPads and loosening paper jams in printers. They sat on a pile of feed sacks, leaning back against the weathered barn wall. It was not the most comfortable place to relax, but the marijuana took away any sharp edges and hard lumps.

It was a real barn with real Brown Swiss cows watching them with wide eyes and snorting their disapproval. He and Ruba had taken her sister's kids to the petting zoo last summer and he had spent almost five dollars in feed from the coin dispensers. Here was the real deal. Jasir had never seen real cows up close or ridden a horse or lay in a barn to smoke weed.

"Kayla's good-looking, man," Brian said, inhaling and holding it for a few seconds. "If I wasn't married I might have asked her out."

Jasir pictured Kayla's small, tight ass in her drab green nurse's scrubs. He carefully took the burning joint and gently pinched it between his fingers. He was worried the cows would get high, too. They watched him with intermittent and disinterested snorts.

His divorce was almost finalized; he and Ruba had another mediation before heading to court. They had spent more time separating than being married—almost two months after their honeymoon in Punta Cana where the ocean lapped against their shins as they sat on the beach, their arms buttressed behind them, never touching each other. He had wanted to say something romantic about the sunset, how there would never be another one like it, but a perpetual clot of self-contempt lodged in his throat had obstructed his speech.

He knew she had married him to conceal her indiscretions. She wasn't a virgin—he had known this, too, before he and his parents went to formally request her hand. They had gone to high school together and he was in love with her then, and the same feelings washed over him like a fresh coat of paint the day seven years later he bumped into her at Starbucks. Still beautiful, she had become sexy now, had outgrown her girlishness. She had given him her number when he asked.

After only a few months, she insisted they get engaged, and with his parents' tentative blessings, Jasir stood before Ruba's parents, awkwardly shaking hands with Ruba's mother who had appeared relieved but not happy.

While the sheikh blessed their engagement, he caught Ruba's father watching him sternly, their close relatives praying with lowered heads in front of their faces. Jasir was convinced he loved her and he clung to her like a kid clutching a deflated soccer ball. Deep in his heart, he was equally convinced she did not love him and had simply settled. She smiled at him in a manner of remembering to be polite, and during their first year of marriage Jasir found most of her gestures were practiced reactions to him as though she had been trained to be a dutiful wife. She had no natural inclination to be near him and seemed to be measuring out affection and attentiveness like preparing a precise mixture of ingredients to ensure a cake did not collapse after it had risen, though it turned out to be utterly tasteless.

Then the calls in the middle of night. Her cellphone hummed on the nightstand and she'd immediately snatch it up, checking the number, glancing over her shoulder to see if Jasir was awake, and he pretended he was sleeping. He knew it was the same man who'd broken her heart, who'd thrown her away.

"He wants me back," Ruba told him on a night it had taken him two hours to get home from work during an ice storm. He'd driven below the speed limit, witnessing several spin-outs and crashes along the way. He'd been relieved to step safely inside their townhouse, sparsely decorated though they'd lived in it for a year. He'd been more interested in painting and hanging pictures than Ruba had been. She'd nod or shake her head when he'd point to large mirror or hold up a ceramic vase as they strolled through the housewares floor of a department store. They never held hands as they shopped. Jasir occasionally touched her shoulder and was happy when she let his hand linger when she stopped to feel a plush throw pillow, bringing it to her cheek.

"Why did you go through with it?" Brian suddenly asked him, taking the joint. "I mean, you had a feeling, right? Why didn't you call it off?"

"I thought it was cold feet or something," Jasir said.

"I don't know, man," Brian said. "You should've been able to tell a thing like that." He exhaled long and hard.

The cows flicked their tails, but otherwise stood perfectly still.

"Anyway, you should ask Kayla out, man. You have to move on sometime," Brian told him.

Jasir closed his eyes and it was easy to drown out Brian and the cold barn and the smell of cow shit. Only Ruba's image floated behind his eyelids like clouds in time lapse. For a little while, it felt good seeing her body unfettered by gravity, moving across his screen of consciousness. But, then he felt his arms and legs grow heavy and his stomach sank and he was worried his internal organs would tear through his asshole.

* * *

Lloyd woke them up at four-thirty a.m. The temperature had dropped almost ten degrees overnight and the ground felt wet and firm under Jasir's boots.

Jasir hadn't known that deer were colorblind or how it was best to hit a target near the front shoulder where the heart was centered. He hadn't considered where a deer's heart was positioned. There was plenty of stuff he hadn't known, like how Ruba had called an attorney the day after they returned from Punta Cana and how she was obligated to return the muhir—the ring and gold jewelry dowry—as part of tradition, his mother had insisted. But, Jasir did not want any of it.

They walked a half-mile into a thicket then stopped at the edge of a clearing to set up Lloyd's blind. It was made of camouflaged rayon with two collapsible chairs. Brian carried an extra stool for Jasir. The three men fit snugly inside like overgrown kids in a tent. Lloyd poured plastic mugs of freshly roasted coffee from a thermos and the aroma enveloped Jasir and warmed the shelter.

Jasir sat a few inches lower than the two other men and as straight as he could to peer from the cutout windows of the blind. He felt strangely alone and isolated, staring ahead. He refrained from speaking. Brian sipped his coffee and rolled his head to get the kinks out of his neck. His uncle Lloyd drank his coffee and refilled his mug. When the thermos was empty, he popped chocolate M&M's in his mouth. The three of them waited in silence.

Soon, wisps of pink and orange appeared low in the trees and everything seemed hazy to Jasir. It was almost six a.m. when a doe trotted into the clearing. Lloyd tapped Brian's knee and Brian in turn nudged Jasir, a finger at his lips.

The doe looked like the ones Jasir had seen when driving near forest preserves on LaGrange Road. There were usually two or three of them foraging for food, sometimes so close to the shoulder he could see their glassy eyes.

The doe scratched the ground, one hoof suspended in mid-air as she stopped to listen for alien sounds. As he watched it, Jasir imagined Ruba scuffling in oversized fluffy slippers from their bed to the master bathroom where he knew she was cleaning him off of her, wiping away his cum so it would not drench her insides. She had become adept at swiveling away from his body like she was tumbling out of a wrecked car to flag someone down who could sweep her away to safety.

Pawing at the ground with its hoof, the doe dipped its nose in a damp pile of leaves. Its neck was short but elegant.

Jasir had not fully explored Ruba's body, had not licked her skin so her pores would open up to him and he could infuse them with his heat. On some nights, she had permitted him the nape of her neck—or maybe she hadn't been awake—and he delicately shifted her wavy black hair to one shoulder and kissed the knob of her spine, the spot lovers might ignore or find unappealingly bony. It was Jasir's favorite part of her.

Lloyd shifted his weight and nodded at Brian who handed him a rifle. The doe froze a moment then resumed its foraging. Lloyd's shoulders quivered as he silently belched.

"Jesus," Brian whispered. He nudged Jasir's arm.

They watched as a four by six white-tailed buck trotted into the clearing, alert and dignified. It was the most impressive thing Jasir had ever seen. Its coat was brownish-gray with hints of summer red. It stood almost seven feet and its antlers looked like they could gouge a man's throat. The tines curved inward like a disembodied rib cage.

Before Jasir could utter awe or praise, another buck entered the scene as if on cue. It took cautious steps towards the first deer, sizing it up. It, too, possessed a handsome set of antlers, a scrubbed-down tannish hue.

"Jesus," Brian whispered again.

Lloyd had not flinched and vaguely nodded his head as though silently working out a problem. He set the butt of his rifle down in front of him and leaned against it with both hands, weighing the scene.

The first buck had a thicker neck and instinctively wagged its tail, revealing its white underside. It scraped its hoof and reared its bifurcated antlers.

The doe took a few steps back, forming a triangle among the three of them. It stood still and watched as Jasir and the other men did from the blind.

The bucks edged closer and Jasir could see a dark thick line running down the nose of each one as they bent their antlers. They clacked against each other then hastily pulled back for several seconds before the first buck stabbed more vigorously. It soon locked into the smaller buck's antlers and held strong. The doe appeared more alarmed as the clacking grew louder. When the smaller one managed to disengage itself, it scampered backwards then galloped away into the thicket.

Before the first buck could enjoy its victory, Lloyd seized the moment and shot it broadside through its right shoulder. Jasir instinctively clapped his hands over his ears.

In a blink, the doe sprinted away. The buck collapsed with a heavy thud and tried to stand again. Its rear hooves clawed at the ground and with all of its might, it lifted itself up, its front legs trembling above an imaginary earthquake. It collapsed again and a quiet calm draped the clearing. The buck's former glory had seeped away with its blood.

"That was fucking amazing," Jasir said. It was victory and defeat, all at once. He had been rooting for the first buck. Then Jasir felt a pang of dread. It was over. He quickly dismissed it, savoring the exhilaration that had overcome his exhaustion. He felt like he was drawing breath for the first time that morning, the adrenaline pooling his lungs. He had not shot the deer himself, but he had absorbed the cold tension that hovered over the rivals as they sparred in the clearing. All of his senses were keener and his heart pounded with ferocity. He stood up with his rifle and aimed at a tree trunk, knowing but not caring that he looked ridiculous. He needed to hold the rifle steady, to breathe in through his nostrils and exhale through his mouth as though drawing a bead on a real target.

Lloyd was busy measuring the buck with a retractable roll of tape, recording its dimensions in a tiny notebook he had tucked in his front shirt pocket.

"What're you doing, man?" Brian said, slapping Jasir on the shoulder, startling him out of his reverie.

There was a screech, then a scratchy thud on the clearing. A red-shouldered hawk lay twitching where the doe had stood frozen earlier. It was several yards away from the deer carcass which had stopped moving.

Jasir's hands felt electrified from the discharge of the rifle, his veins throbbing with terror. He moved slowly toward the felled hawk. The bullet from Jasir's rifle had torn through its right wing, shearing feathers from the spot as though it had been perversely plucked, and in its tapestry was an awful gaping hole.

"Jesus Christ," Brian said. "Shit, man."

Jasir felt nauseous. The adrenaline that had been coursing through him thickened and slowed as he stared at the wounded hawk, hopping around in a grotesque dance. Its good wing stretched out in a strange and defiant dignity. As it slowed down and twitched, Jasir dropped to his knees and reached out to touch it.

"It's still kicking," Lloyd said. "Damn shame." He pulled out a .177 pellet pistol and tapped Jasir's shoulder with it. "Finish it, son. Put it out of its misery."

Brian took a step back, giving Jasir space to stand and fire down on the hawk. "Right in its head, man," he instructed Jasir.

Jasir nodded and lifted himself up from the ground, every limb suddenly clumsy and any move he made was cumbersome with the weight of bone, muscle and blood. He took the pistol and it became a strange extension of his hand like a new evolutionary appendage sprouted for this precise moment.

He stood over the hawk, its skittish and unhinged body parallel to the deer carcass, which vacantly stared back. Ruba in her mermaid wedding dress entered his mind and escaped into the recesses of his brain where humans stored images—useless and innocuous—until occasion called to retrieve them, like the scent of gardenia perfume infusing the nostrils or the tartness of raspberries on the tongue.

Jasir aimed, unsure whether he could hit the small target of a head, even at close range. Maybe he should aim for the heart instead, still pumping beneath a greater expanse of flesh that he could not possibly miss. Or maybe the creature would simply succumb and stop twitching.

"Son, it's suffering," Lloyd said. "Shoot it."

"C'mon, man," Brian joined in. "Just do it."

"Okay," Jasir heard himself say. He didn't want it to suffer any longer.

Before the other men could coax him again, Jasir fired twice and it was over. The hawk stopped twitching and there was no movement except for the rippling breeze through its good wing, creating a soft rustle barely audible if not for Jasir and the men standing still.

Lloyd lifted the unmarred wing. "Looks like four feet," he said. "Damn shame."

Jasir nodded. He didn't need a measuring tape. He could tell its wingspan just by looking at it.

New And Gently Used Hijab

Sometimes Iman knew these arabiyat who sat across from her desk, applying for food stamps. She'd seen them in line at Jerusalem Bakery on 95th Street, buying cans of hummus and a dozen pocket bread with crumpled single dollar bills. Or she recognized them from weekly mosque classes where other villagers, transplanted like them in America, could find some solace in the company of clanswomen while reciting Qur'an together. Iman might nod at them or give them a small wave; most times she usually pretended she hadn't noticed them, saving them their dignity, but they seemed glad to see her.

In her office, Iman translated the application for public aid and showed these women where to sign on the forms. She watched them delicately press a pen, with a logo wrapped around it, along the solid line. They looked anxious, carefully signing their names in English like children learning cursive for the first time under the watchful eye of a teacher. They prayed out loud that—inshallah—the State of Illinois would not deny them so their husbands would not have to find more work and be away more hours from their cramped apartments lining Ridgeland Avenue. They told Iman that this was not what they had expected when they came to the States.

Iman suspected some of the arabiyat did not have a legitimate need, but were pressured by scheming husbands who claimed to be religious men yet felt no remorse abusing the system.

"He swears this government is full of kuffar," one woman unwittingly told Iman, scratching her hijab and blowing her nose into a rumpled tissue. A dark-eyed boy tugged at the woman's purse. "How can it be a sin to take wealth from sinners?" she asked Iman. She slapped her son's hand away from her purse. "Bas! Enough!"

Other times, Iman wished she did not know the woman fidgeting in the worn leather chair across from her, one eye swollen to the color of a ripened purple fig, or broken lips with scabs like the skin of plums. But, Palestinian clans ran deep and extended far like sewer trenches in a refugee camp. Iman swallowed her shame as she gently listed the things the women could purchase with their LINK card: baby formula, toothpaste, milk. Birth control pills were not eligible.

Still, Iman found that these women possessed a pure kind of grace that made them forget their own dire circumstances and to turn their attention on her and ask through busted lips about Iman's mother and how her gallbladder surgery had gone, or whether her twin sons would be starting preschool soon. When the appointment was over they always said, *Inshallah khair. Good things will come.* And Iman found herself grateful for this indomitable optimism. It somehow made it easier to show up for work every day.

Twenty years ago, SERVICES FOR ARAB FAMILIES opened the door of its tiny office next to an appliance warranty center. It sat in an industrial area near the Bridgeview mosque and a UPS central shipping plant. The agency's skeletal staff had been devoted to assisting immigrant families in the Chicago area navigate bureaucracy. Iman had been working there for six years, and she was proud to celebrate SFAF's upcoming twentieth anniversary.

An idea struck her one morning as she watched her coworker Salwa tuck a cellphone into her hijab, where it disappeared against Salwa's ear. It protruded in a rectangular outline like a pack of cigarettes rolled deeply above the bicep of a t-shirt. With free hands, Salwa could begin filing folders while reprimanding her teenage son who was in charge of two younger sisters at home. Amused, Iman observed the scene and wondered how Salwa's voice managed to flow up through her hidden cellphone.

"Wallah, wallah, if you don't stop pestering your sister, I'll call your father," Salwa threatened. She shuffled papers and searched for a pen.

A whiny, faraway voice came back through the speaker. "Mama, it's Renahs' fault."

Salwa looked up at Iman and made a scribbling motion with her fingers. Iman reached over Salwa's desk, carefully pulled out the top drawer that was nearly obstructed by Salwa's swollen belly and fished out a bundle of pens.

"I'm sorry," Salwa mouthed to Iman. After a few more minutes of scolding her son, she gave him a stern goodbye and stood up. "Samhini, Iman," she said, rubbing her lower back. "At six months, I'm operating on half a brain." She looked at the pens. "Now, where did I leave my phone?"

Iman pointed to her coworker's ear and Salwa threw her head back and laughed. "I told you," she said. "Half a brain." Salwa extracted her phone from her headscarf and an idea dawned on Iman.

"What do you think of hijab donations? Iman asked Salwa. A collection drive for headscarves?"

"Mashallah! That's a great idea!" Salwa beamed at her. She rubbed her belly in small circles.

"I don't think the agency has ever done anything like it," Iman said. Satisfaction bloomed in her chest as she jotted down contacts to make. A few of the arabiyat she'd assisted this week wore fraying headscarves and likely considered purchasing new hijab more than a little frivolous when there were bills to pay. Other clothing donations would be welcome, too, but a hijab drive was an exclusive gift for the wives and mothers who'd placed their own needs behind their families'. From her squeaky swivel chair, Salwa leaned as far over as she could to file a stack of folders in a noisy metal cabinet. "I think it's a great idea," she declared again. She pressed a fist to her mouth and belched.

By noon, Iman found a generous printer to design flyers with a silhouette of a woman wearing a headscarf, her arms raised in praise to the sky. And she arranged for the Bridgeview Mosque to host the event in its parking lot. They would set up long tables for collection, and if it rained, they could move indoors to a community room.

Happily, she motioned for a woman in a black abaya to have a seat at her desk. The woman had been standing outside the office, waiting for someone to open the agency at eight o'clock.

"I can't afford a babysitter," she explained to Iman, sitting upright, dark eyes in a pale face. The wide sleeves of her abaya cascaded down her thin wrists as she spoke. "I need to get back before my little ones wake up."

Iman nodded and swiveled her chair to face her computer screen. She pulled her cellphone from her purse which she kept stored in a filing drawer in her desk. After her first appointment she would call her mother's home to check in on her sons. She glanced at a clock on the wall near Salwa's desk; she might catch them before their mid-morning nap. Outside the office, the sliding door of a UPS truck slammed shut and a few moments later, an engine roared to life.

* * *

It was a perfect day for the drive—not too warm for early June. A few innocuous clouds streaked the sky.

The Bridgeview Mosque was a small building with a tiny weather-beaten black dome and minaret. Its windows were its most impressive feature: the arched frames held turquoise stained-glass panels. There were separate entrances for men and women; children indiscriminately entered through either pair of the heavy double-doors until puberty.

Twenty volunteers showed up for the drive including Salwa's children who carried empty boxes to the tables for filling. Kifah, an agent who had been at SFAF the longest, moved around the parking lot, waving at people with a clipboard. She peeped under each table, bracing hand against thigh, making sure there were water bottles and snacks for the volunteers. She wore a hijab with a blue and pink floral pattern like a Monet painting. Her long navy-blue abaya flared over her hips and her short, squat stature was like a bell slowly tolling when she walked.

"Sabah el khair, ya habayib," she called out. "Good morning, my darlings. May Allah bestow all of His blessings upon you for the good work you're doing today."

"Sabah el noor, ya Sayida Kifah," the adult volunteers rang back like students performing rote. They sipped from their coffee mugs and engaged in minor gossip while they awaited the first drop-off.

Most donations came from arabiyat zooming into the lot and quickly handing over a plastic grocery bag of scarves while their children screamed in the backseat. A few of the women were the same clients Iman had helped fill out welfare forms. They showed up on foot, pushing a baby in a stroller and straddling a toddler on their hip. It was proof again of their unwavering optimism and that they conceived their lot was not the worst—elhamdulillah.

The steady stream of donations pleased Iman and even Salwa managed almost a full day before plopping down in a portable folding chair. Her heavy lactating breasts pressed against the top of her belly when she sat.

During the last hour, a black Dodge Ram pulled up and parked on the curb. Iman stopped folding a pile of scarves and saw an old white woman cautiously hop down from the passenger side. She opened the gate of the truck's flat bed and carried a large box toward Iman's donation table.

"Yazen!" Iman called to Salwa's son. "Help that lady!"

The old white woman handed Yazen the box and lightly tapped his shoulder in gratitude. She followed him to the table.

"I saw a flyer at Tony's Supermarket," she explained to Iman. "I spoke to some of my girlfriends and they managed to give me a little something to bring here today." She gestured around the parking lot. "For your cause."

"How generous of you," Iman said, examining the contents of the box.

Amarkan never ceased to amaze her.

The white woman clasped her liver-spotted hands on the edge of the box as Iman riffled through sweaters, long skirts and a half-dozen fancy scarves with paisley designs and bold geometric shapes. They looked like the ones fashionably draped around the mannequins at Macy's.

"I hope these will do," the woman said. She removed her sunglasses and looked at Iman with milky blue eyes. Her silver hair was neatly trimmed in a pixie and Iman could tell she had once been an attractive woman.

"They're great, ma'am. Thank you very much." Iman was glad for new ones, let alone stylish ones. Not all of them were long enough to cover a woman's head. At any rate, the arabiyat in need would make use of anything and not let a single piece of fabric go to waste—Iman was certain of this. She filled out a tax-exempt receipt while the white woman prattled on.

"My son drove me," she told Iman. "That's him, waiting in the truck."

Iman tore off the perforated slip from a pad.

"Mark served in I-rack and Afghan-uh-stan," the old woman continued. "Three tours of duty. I'm so relieved he's home now. Can you imagine how scared I was when he was gone? And for what? Some precious oil."

Iman politely smiled and nodded at the woman's bitter words, but stayed quiet. She extended the receipt, but the white woman, still clutching the box, ignored it and leaned closer to Iman like she was about to divulge a secret. Iman quickly glanced over the woman's shoulder. Her son did not turn to look at them and stared past the hood of the truck. Uneasiness tugged at Iman's chest and she looked over at Salwa whose eyes were closed and hands peacefully folded across her belly.

"He tells me things when he's had too many beers," the white woman whispered loudly to Iman. "I can't shut him down, but I don't want to listen, either. What can I do? I'm his mother."

Iman held the slip of paper and listened. A few more cars had pulled up to make a deposit, and she vaguely heard the cheerful greetings pouring out of rolled-down windows. The drivers were happy to have made it before the donation drive was over.

"What's your name, dear?" the white woman asked her.

"Iman."

"That's lovely. Does it mean anything?"

"Faith," Iman said. "It means faith."

"That's lovely, dear," the woman said again, tapping her long acrylic fingernails on the box flap. She fingered the button of a salmon-colored sweater inside the box.

"I thought if I did this, it would be good for Mark. You know, for his spirit, she said. Joanne left him a month ago and won't let him see their son. Joanne—that's his wife—found a sock in his duffel bag. It was full of hair. They were from the beards of men. Tally-ban who were killed." The deep wrinkles around the woman's eyes and mouth rippled in distress. "Can you believe it, dear?"

Iman shook her head dumbly. She'd sat with her husband, evening after evening, year after year, watching *Al Jazeera* satellite news, making sure the twins were asleep before inviting the images of dead children, their bodies burned and battered by explosions, into her living room. War had still been distant to her, despite the uncensored carnage she could easily access with a click of a remote control. But, now it had suddenly rushed over her like a gale slapping against a once tranquil beach, dredging up sand and displacing seashells. Death and destruction had become as palpable as the cardboard boxes, the tape dispensers, the hundreds of scarves splayed across the donation tables. Her throat closed and it was her turn to clutch the white woman's box. She needed to keep steady, unsure what to do next. She looked again at Salwa who blithely dozed amidst the clamor of young volunteers laughing loudly as they finished sealing boxes. The imam in a skullcap gestured to them to lower their voices as he shuffled inside the mosque to lead the dusk prayer.

The white woman lifted a sleeve from the box and hid her fingers inside its knitted wrist. She looked beseechingly at Iman.

"It's a terrible thing, I know, but it's important to forgive in this life. You know this, dear. Your name means faith, right? You said so." As she spoke, the woman's eyes brimmed with tears and flowed down her face. Her lips puckered and the wrinkles around her mouth looked like dry and cracked mud. "If we can't forgive, how can we go on? We have to believe we can do better. Isn't that right, dear?"

"I don't know," Iman said. She was not sure she had uttered it out loud, or if it had been a whisper like the rustling of the trees as the sun began its decline. The lower rim of the sky turned flaming orange then pink. Car headlights came on at the stop signs on each corner of the block. The turquoise windows of the mosque soaked the dying light, turning them opal

Despite her heavy abaya, Iman felt cold. She looked past the white woman and at her son, his hands gripping the steering wheel, as though keeping him anchored inside the car.

"Men do ugly things," the woman said, dabbing at her face with a tissue paper she had pulled from an oversized leather purse—too heavy it seemed to Iman for the woman's frail wrist to bear. "What they think is for the common good." She loudly blew her nose, her pale skin turned blotchy and miserable. "Well, I hope this helps your cause," she said.

She caressed the clothes once more like a farewell to one reposed in a coffin. Then she turned the flaps of the box down and slowly ambled away. Her son never once looked in Iman's direction. He gunned the engine and drove off.

"Mashallah! That's the biggest load we've gotten." Kifah beamed at Iman's elbow, pointing with a tape dispenser that replaced her clipboard. "I think we can call it a day! Look at poor Salwa! Ya haram!" She squeezed Iman's shoulder and returned to sealing boxes on each long table.

Iman looked around. They had collected over three hundred scarves. She had never seen this many hijab in one place. A few scarves swathed the end of Iman's table in a loose and wild heap like they had just been pulled off and discarded by tired arabiyat after a long day in public.

She pulled back the flaps of the white woman's box and fished for the expensive and stylish scarves. They were mostly gently used except for one with a price tag still attached. The old woman's contribution alone would help a dozen arabiyat. But, they had suddenly become tainted to Iman, touched by an old white woman whose son had killed Muslims, had scoffed at and desecrated the corpses. She rubbed the silky fabric between her thumb and fingers then dropped them back in, grabbed a tape dispenser and sealed the box. It was much lighter than she expected when she carried it to the rear of the mosque and tossed it into a giant dumpster. The stench of half-eaten lunches and soured milk hovered above the rim.

As she walked back to the parking lot, the evening breeze picked up the hem of her abaya and the soft fabric swayed around her ankles. Iman considered what the white woman had said about her name—about having faith. She turned the corner and hoped Allah might someday bequeath her with a bit of grace, too.

IF I'M NOT HOME

Nizar wondered what the doctor saw when he ran an MRI on his father's brain. He imagined the synapses shriveled like dried grape vines suffering a long drought. But he knew other patches were still lush with vitality, nourishing his father's long-term memories. Nizar could see them like bubbling springs, and just before his father spoke and revealed the setting of his boyhood village or an event that happened his first year in Chicago, Nizar envisioned them spilling over and rushing into every recess of the old man's brain. A familiar glint of sheer joy—sometimes, searing pain—flickered in his father's eyes before he told his story. Across lobes of gray stuff, robust veins still fiercely throbbed with images of life—those that counted to his father.

The old man could not recall having just eaten, but he gave painstaking eyewitness details about the yahood—curiously blonde and blue-eyed—storming his village with automatic rifles when he was only six years old. His father remembered when Nizar and Lamise were born, how he was happy to have a girl first so she wouldn't be bullied by an older brother.

And there were secrets, too, his father remembered, pulsating just below the surface of consciousness. Like when he found love letters Nizar's mother had buried deep in an old suitcase she kept hidden under their bed. They were from some arrabi man who had attended Bir Zeit University with her. The details surrounding the affair were still nebulous to Nizar, yet this man became a palpable presence one day in his childhood like the sudden appearance of snow in early March when the sidewalks had been clear for weeks. For ten years, the man had been writing to his mother. Seven and nine years old, Nizar and Lamise had come home one late afternoon from summer camp at Garfield Park just a few blocks from their two-story house. In the gangway, they could hear their father shouting in Arabic and his mother's muffled responses.

Lamise had quickly grabbed Nizar's hand. *It's okay, Zee-Zee*, she consoled him when he began to cry. They waited in the backyard, sitting on the hot grass that stuck to their sweaty thighs, until the front door slammed and they knew their father was gone.

Their mother was seated at the kitchen table holding a package of frozen lima beans over one side of her face.

Hello, habibi! she cooed. *Bas, bas! Enough crying, Zee-Zee! Everything's fine.*

She hugged him close and Nizar breathed in his mother's scent—a combination of Pine Sol cleaner and baharat—a blend of savory spices she sprinkled on roasted lamb and vegetables. She pressed the frozen beans against his back when she embraced him, and it felt good after being in the hot sun.

Now go wash your face and hands.

Nizar remembered stopping at the door of his parents' bedroom. Inside, letters were shredded and strewn across the rust-colored carpet. The old blue suitcase was tossed open near a dresser, its silky lining detached and frayed. To a young Nizar, it had looked like the mouth of a whale. He lifted several strips of paper, examining the mysterious language he could only loosely speak when his parents asked him questions, but which he could never read or write. He was terrified by the weight of such letters and the words they bore that would throw his father into a rage and cause him to hurt Nizar's mother.

That night Nizar dreamt his mother had sewn the torn strands of the letters back to their original form and clipped each one with a single wooden pin to the clothesline in the backyard. Their white neighbors came over to read the letters and though Nizar was conscious in the dream that they were amarkan and could not possibly read Arabic, he saw their lips moving, silently formulating the words as they moved from one hanging letter to the next.

* * *

Nizar was twenty-four years old when his mother suggested there was something wrong with his father.

This morning, he was trying to put on my girdle, he had overheard her telling his sister Lamise, newly married, on the phone. *I've been noticing little things like that.* His mother spoke in a medini dialect—euphonious and elegant. His father was a fellah from El Bireh and he had always sounded crude in the presence of her family.

He didn't tell his mother or sister that only a few nights before, his father had been unable to start the car after they locked up their liquor store.

What's wrong, Baba? Nizar asked, fastening his seatbelt. He waved at

Marcus, one of their clerks as he walked in the opposite direction of the car. A hooting laughter and a bottle breaking echoed down the block of run-down houses. It had been April and an unusually warm night in Chicago and Nizar rolled down his window. *Did you drop your keys?*

His father looked dumbly at his hands, which were tightly gripping the steering wheel.

Nizar fished around the console, lifting a half-empty can of Dr. Pepper from a cup-holder as though the keys could be hidden beneath it.

I can't. I don't know how, his father finally said. In the car's dark interior, a low sob shook his father's shoulders.

Nizar sat frozen. It was a terrible moment of revelation—still worse than his father mistaking his mother's clothes for his own. The first thread of self-sufficiency had been yanked and the months to follow began a steady unraveling of a once fierce and commanding man. Their roles would be switched when Nizar's mother left them later—Nizar the adult caretaker, his father a helpless child. As the days passed, it broke Nizar's heart to witness the spectacle of his father trying to force his foot into the wrong shoe or fumbling for the names of the oldest clerks at the store, ones his father had trained himself. They, too, were disheartened by the old man's descent.

But his mother and sister could not understand that. To them, he had become an inconvenience, like having to constantly chase after a rambunctious child who wanted to grab everything off supermarket shelves if you were not paying close attention.

Since she left two years ago, his mother dutifully called every Sunday morning. In Nablus, it was nearly evening due to the eight-hour difference in time zones, and Nizar pictured her sitting in his grandparents' enclosed verandah, looking out onto the main street. She had grown up with loquat and almond trees, raised *bil iz*—a blissful childhood in spite of the Occupation. Her father was a mukhtar—a well-respected mayor of Nablus. Nizar, Lamise and his mother spent half the summer there until high school when Nizar began working at his father's store in Roseland.

"How's Baba?" His mother's voice was saturated with politeness and cheer. It was a vague, disinterested question like she had just asked Nizar about the chili pepper plant she had abandoned in a giant urn on the tiny patio of their townhouse.

"Baba's fine," Nizar said brusquely. "Do you want to talk to him?" From thousands of miles away, he wanted his mother to feel the sharp sting of shame. It had been one betrayal after another, each in its own time unearthed to Nizar and Lamise when they were old enough to understand. Still, he hadn't fully comprehended the implications of infidelity. It was like his childhood friend Basheer explaining rudimentary sex to him when he was nine years old. Nizar had tried hard to visualize such an outlandish act as he sat cross-legged underneath the basketball rim attached to his friend's garage

The word *cheat* as in *to be unfaithful to a spouse* had never been uttered in front of them and Nizar wondered if an Arabic word existed. He had heard *ghesh* used to describe what one of his father's friends did on his taxes, or when they had played checkers, Nizar's father would teasingly call him a *ghesh-shash*—a cheater—though he let Nizar win every time.

But, there was no familiar word to describe an infidelity, only ugly names his father had called his mother over the years, standing close to her as she stirred a pot at the stove, hissing in her ear, or in the car driving home from family dinner parties, pounding his fist on the vinyl dashboard. These names had made Nizar cringe in shame at the time, though he had no part in his mother's actions. And, now she had done it again—cheated his father by leaving for good. Despite all of it, his father still remembered his deep love for Nizar's mother. At the sound of her voice long distance, he wept and Nizar could hear her consoling him through the mouthpiece.

"Let me chat with you first, Zee-Zee," his mother said. "How's the store?"

"Busy as always." He didn't tell her that another child was struck and killed by a car at the intersection outside the liquor store. It was the third one in two years. A pastor from one of the parishes in Roseland had asked Nizar to sign a petition to get a traffic light with a surveillance camera installed on 87th and Loomis Street. *If it was white kids getting hit, you'd bet there'd be something already done about it,* he had complained to Nizar.

"I heard your friend Jabra is getting engaged," his mother said. "Mabrook!"

Nizar sat at the dinette table and gazed out onto the patio. Three inches of snow were packed hard against the bottom of the sliding door. Snow was also on the armrests and seats of the wicker chairs. Bare stalks of his mother's pepper plant remained in one urn. He stopped watering it when she postponed her return home for a second time. That was two years ago. In her absence, the peppers were no longer like vibrant Christmas lights against a pine tree, but had shriveled and turned yellowish-brown until they broke off. In other pots she had planted mint leaves and pungent geraniums. Last spring, the rabbits ate them up and Nizar watched them one morning and did not disturb them.

He listened as his mother masterfully redirected the conversation. "What about you, Zee-Zee? When do you plan on settling down? There are lovely girls here."

Nizar wanted to hang up then but he didn't have the courage. On some level, he still loved his mother as a child dutifully does. He blamed her for his fearing the love of a woman, for perceiving marriage as conveniently settling for someone—when time had run out to be with the one you really wanted. He didn't want to have kids who were forced to carry grown-up secrets. He remembered the year he'd been part of a conspiracy against his father.

* * *

Months after the shredded love letters, things seemed to return to normal. Nizar's parents spoke and laughed as they always had though his father's eyes became fretful when his mother left the kitchen to throw out the garbage or to bring in the laundry hanging off the clothesline in the backyard. This, in turn, made Nizar anxious as he waited for his father to pounce as soon as his mother stepped through the back door. He hated what his father made him feel inside—stony walls closing in on his lungs, threatening to crush them like in an *Indiana Jones* movie. At the very last conceivable moment, his mother returned with a wide smile and a hamper of fresh towels and undershirts, and the walls mercifully halted, inches from mashing his lungs.

When Nizar entered the third grade, his mother began a ritual of coming home late in the afternoon, an hour or two after he and Lamise had been sitting in front of the television set, watching re-runs of *The Brady Bunch* and *Happy Days*.

If I'm not home when you get there, just eat cereal. I won't be long, she advised them when she pulled their station wagon to the curb of their grade school. A line of cars softly honked goodbyes to children as they scampered out of vinyl back seats and flooded the playground. Teachers waved them over, assembling students in unkempt, but discernible lines.

This happened at least twice a week. Some days she was there when Nizar and Lamise tore through the back door, but they knew she had just gotten home because she was still wearing a pair of tan pantyhose and a tweed skirt with a ruffle blouse. By the door, her leather pumps looked like they had been hastily kicked off her feet. Other days, Lamise carefully poured each of them a bowl of Frosted Flakes and they ate silently on the couch, waiting for their mother.

Hello, my little chicks, she'd sing as soon as she entered. Her eyes were shining bright and a flush of happiness swept across her cheeks. *How are my soosan?*

Seeing her this way, Nizar was filled with instant relief.

When winter blanketed the city with heavy snow, she would be much later getting home. A few days before their holiday break, Nizar's father sat stiffly between them like an awkward, overgrown child as they watched *A Charlie Brown Christmas*. It was nearly seven-thirty when they heard the turn of the knob.

Ya Allah! How horrible the traffic! she proclaimed when she saw the expression on his father's face. *I was a fool to even go out to Sears today!*

She pulled off each finger of her plum-colored suede gloves and unwrapped her matching wool scarf. She moved through the family room, unbuttoning her coat while gathering their bowls and spoons from the coffee table.

You're home early, Hameed, she said casually. *Are you hungry, kids?*

Before they could spring off the couch, his father said, *Stay right here, ya loolad.*

Nizar and Lamise sat frozen. His father stood up and swiftly grabbed his wife's arm and pulled her toward their bedroom. She dropped the bowls on the counter and they clattered hard, but did not break.

Their mother looked back at them with a small, but consoling smile, still wearing her coat.

As soon as their father slammed the door, Lamise hopped off the couch and scampered on tiptoe into the hallway. She sat on the floor, her ear pressed up against the door, which was unnecessary because their father was shouting.

Why hasn't the professor come for you? Ha? his father demanded. *Because he is only using you, you sharmoota!*

Nizar's heart was thumping wildly in his throat. He winced at the insult, not knowing what it meant except that it was a terrible thing to be calling his mother.

How come he didn't marry you to begin with? Tell me—why didn't he? his father raged, not giving his mother a chance to reply before firing the next question.

Where is this smart-ass ustaz of yours? He's a goddamn coward and thief!

There was a shattering of glass and Nizar and Lamise jumped. He clutched his sister's elbow and began whimpering.

Quiet! Lamise whispered hotly in his face.

He drew his knees up to his chest and sniffled into them. While his father stomped around her, Nizar pictured his mother sitting erect on the edge of the bed and fingering the *oonsah* around her neck—the golden charm containing the silhouette of a young woman. Its rectangular frame was scalloped and etched with tiny incisions, giving it depth and dimension. Many times, Nizar had sat on her lap lifting the *oonsah*, cool and heavy in his palm. He would trace the young woman's head with the tip of his finger.

Your father gave this to me as part of my muhir when he married me, she had once explained, kissing the top of Nizar's head.

* * *

Nizar wondered now if his mother still had the necklace. Did she intend on giving it to Lamise along with her other matrimonial pieces? Or had their value declined as a result of a bad marriage?

On the other end of the line, Nizar's mother idly chatted. She gave him the recent updates on the political climate though he had not asked, speaking like a news reporter from *Al Jazeera*. "It's the seventieth day of hunger strikes in the prisons. No end in sight," she told him.

Nizar asked her about his grandmother who would be ninety-two next month. His mother sounded pleased by the inquiry.

"So, have you met anyone you like? It's time to settle down, habibi," his mother persisted.

"No," Nizar said. "I'm too busy with the store. And Baba."

"What do the doctors say about your father?" she finally asked.

* * *

That summer, Lamise announced her pregnancy. "It's about time," she teased, giving her husband Ali a poke in his ribs. Ali had been one of Nizar's best friends in middle school.

"Mabrook," Nizar said, giving her a hug. They were having pizza and poker night at Lamise's condo where two other couples joined them. It had taken much nagging on his sister's part for Nizar to attend and bring their father along. The young men gathered on the balcony to smoke cigarettes before the first round.

"Inshallah you'll all be blessed next," Ali told the others.

They nodded noncommittally, bluish-gray smoke obscuring their faces.

Nizar peered through the window. In the living room, his father was picking up framed photographs and studying them closely. Still engaged in conversation with her girlfriends, Lamise watched him from the kitchen as he moved around the room, her eyes never leaving him like a store clerk worried a clumsy patron might break an antique vase or a precious china plate.

"Who's this?" his father asked. He was pointing to a black and white photograph of a couple standing in a snow bank.

Lamise squinted. "Oh, that's Sitti and Seedo," she said good-humoredly. "These are your parents, Baba." She walked over to him and held one side of the frame, her other hand on his shoulder. "Mama said that was the year she saw snow for the first time in the bilad. Do you remember the snow, Baba?"

He had that familiar glint in his eyes and spoke excitedly. "All the harra kids built a small snowman and called him Juha. Remember Juha from the folktales I used to tell you and your brother? You loved that idiot Juha." His father laughed then coughed phlegmatically. "Suhad! Wainik, ya Suhad?" His father looked around as though he'd misplaced something. "Where's your mother?"

Lamise's cheerfulness dissolved. She signaled to Nizar. "He's asking about Mom," she said.

Nizar patted his father's back. "Mom is overseas, Baba. Sit over here. We're playing cards."

Ali unfolded the green mat onto the dining table. He was quick to scold anyone whose drink was not on a coaster. "Okay. Who's in this round?"

Nizar's father kept his hands in his lap while Nizar confidentially showed him his cards.

"What do you think, Baba? Which card suites do you want to build?"

Even a kid could play cards, still some of the arrabi men at the table got serious with the slightest etiquette infringement. Nizar could tell they were growing irritated with every comment and question his father posed about the game.

His father had prematurely revealed Nizar's cards twice and Nizar finally withdrew for the remainder of the night. Their annoyance made it too tense for Nizar to continue. He left the table at the end of a round and assisted his father to a leather recliner. Nizar turned on the television set and they both stared at a young woman on the widescreen, singing very poorly in a competition while the judges scoffed.

As the other men played, Nizar vaguely listened to the chatter of his sister and the other women in the kitchen as they exchanged pregnancy anecdotes and hushed jokes. When his sister laughed she sounded like his mother, high-pitched and like falling rain.

* * *

Two years ago, she'd told Nizar and Lamise she would be gone for just the summer.

"I'll be back before Ramadan begins," his mother had promised. She'd purchased special linens and flannel robes for his grandmother from Target and Kohl's.

The morning after Lamise drove her to O'Hare International Airport, he'd gone into his parents' bedroom to help his father get dressed as his mother had done everyday. He pulled out a dry-cleaned button down shirt and removed it from the plastic. He pushed hangers back and forth for a pair of pants and suddenly stopped.

His mother's side of the closet was almost bare. He ran his hand over a few long sweaters and pantsuits she'd left behind. Icy chunks drifted in his stomach as he yanked a charcoal sweater off the rack, breaking its plastic hanger.

Ramadan had come and gone and his mother still hadn't returned. She'd missed another birthday. He was twenty-seven. In her absence, his father grew increasingly agitated and hostile, lashing out at the black customers that they were dirty and calling Lamise terrible names that made her cry, Nizar knew, when she got into her car. The doctor increased his father's dosage and cautioned Nizar's sister that supervision was extremely important because he was still very mobile.

"You've heard the stories," Lamise told Nizar in private, repeating the doctor's orders. "They find an open door and wander around the neighborhood until someone drives them home—if they're decent people."

"Is she ever coming back?" Nizar asked.

Lamise hadn't looked at him at the time and he realized there had always been an alliance between his sister and his mother. Was his to his father? It seemed natural after all.

"She needs a break, Zee," she said. "Maybe we need to talk about a nursing home."

"Hell no," Nizar snapped. "How the fuck is he going to stay at some place with no Arabs? You think he'll talk to amarkan all day? He isn't disabled.

He can still function. Those places are for the walking dead."

"Zee—"

"Fuck no," Nizar said. "He'll be dead in a year if we dump him in a place like that."

Lamise never broached the subject again. Though she was older than Nizar, he was the only son and brother, and as they grew older the power shifted in his favor. He felt guilty for raising his voice and cursing, but he would not yield.

The second eid passed and his mother sent her holiday regards through his sister. He'd stopped talking to her after that and only now, the year she'd become a grandmother could he muster enough civility for a five-minute phone call.

Lately, Nizar recalled those evenings his mother came home late as he watched his father fumble with the television remote and ask for his wife. He was dressed in a gellabiya that looked like an old-fashioned nightshirt, and over that he wore a fading brown suit jacket. Nizar had seen a photograph of his grandfather dressed the same way, the way old arrabi men did no matter what the occasion—a funeral or wedding. Before he went to the hajj, his father had worn pinstriped, double-breasted suits and woolen sports jackets with suede elbow patches, and he had owned plaid ones during the Seventies when he wore a handle bar mustache. He had worn his favorite tie—blue with wide red stripes—when he and Nizar's mother became U.S. citizens, and on the day they co-signed the mortgage of their first home in Chicago.

Seating feebly on the couch, his father looked like a relic from 1950s Egyptian films. His body was now a mere skeleton, a hanger from which his clothes were lifelessly suspended. Decades ago, his once robust arms and barrel chest had strained against his undershirt when he lifted and tossed Nizar, an enamored young son, into the air. Ripples of loose and sagging skin now hung around his neck like a noose.

"Where's Suhad?" his father would suddenly demand after a long stupor. "Where is that sharmoota? Does she think I don't know what she's been up to?" He would heave himself off the couch and move unsteadily through the kitchen, calling out Nizar's mother's name. Stopping to clutch the edge of the counter or leaning against the doorknob of the bathroom, his father's head lobbed from one side to another in defeat. He seemed to recognize the storage containers arranged on the countertop, the sunflower design scratched and fading. Almost every morning, he removed each lid and peered inside. When his mother hadn't returned after the first year, Lamise emptied the containers of their stale contents—dried sage, mint leaves, and semolina flour. This didn't dissuade his father who continued to inspect them. His mother's dishtowels were still draped over the handle of the oven door, and on a special rack nailed into one wall of the kitchen was a collection of miniature porcelain bells she'd begun when Nizar was in middle school. His father never touched these.

Some days it was easy to quell his father's anger with kind words. Other days, Nizar returned his father's hostility with his own, lashing back at him.

"You're the fool, not me, Baba!" he'd tell his father. "A woman didn't leave me behind. That happened to you, not me." He felt his insides gradually turn callous like dead skin, until soft and hard tones became indistinguishable.

* * *

Nizar could remember his father's face tight with anger, his fists clenched in his lap until the three of them heard the key turn on that night—was it the only time? —she got caught.

On their knees outside their parents' bedroom door, he'd asked his sister, *Who's the professor?*

I don't know. Maybe he was her teacher in the bilad.

But why would Baba be mad at her teacher?

I don't know! she hissed. Shut up! I'm trying to listen.

His mother had emerged unscathed that winter night and she lightly scolded them when she opened the door and found them eavesdropping.

Shoo hatha, ya soosan? What are you doing?

He and Lamise jumped to their feet and she playfully patted their behinds as she chased them back to the family room. They were back in time to see Charlie Brown being lambasted by the other children when he showed up with a scraggly, barren tree for the school pageant.

It was his mother's turn to sit between them, and she breathed softly and twirled her wedding band on her finger. His father had not followed her. He slammed the bathroom door shut behind him and everything was quiet except for the cartoon characters on television and his mother's breathing. His father stayed in the bathroom for a long time.

During the closing credits, he burst out and stood in front of them. His eyes were red and glassy.

Tallak, tallak, tallak! he shouted at his mother. A thread of spit hung from his chin and Nizar waited for him to wipe it away. *Is that what you want?*

Ya sharmoota! Divorce, divorce, divorce! With each repetition he pounded his fist in the air like a gavel. *There—I've said it three times according to el deen! Not that you honor anything, let alone religion!*

His mother stood up and grabbed his father's hands. He yanked them away several times before he allowed her to hold them. He was breathing hard and coughed a little.

Salli a'la el nabi, ya Hameed! Bless your heart, dear man! his mother said, drawing him close. She gently caressed his face and he became quiet. *This family will not fall apart,* she soothed him. *I won't let that ever happen, my love.*

It was like a spell. His father just looked at her then down at Nizar and his sister as though seeing them for the first time. Before his mother could speak again, he rushed out the back door, without his winter coat. In the freezing cold, the car's ignition whined like the discordant tune of a violin until the engine caught, and they heard the sound of tires crunching snow.

His mother sat down again between them. *Don't worry, kids,* she said. *He'll be back.*

* * *

Lamise would be having a boy in January. By October, she had difficulty staying on her feet for too long. Her ankles were swollen and tender, and her face was bloated like she'd been pumped full of steroids. Ali, on constant-call to lift this or move that, had become haggard with his wife's pregnancy. Nizar felt more sorry for his brother-in-law than Lamise.

His mother still called every Sunday and she seemed glad to talk at length about Lamise's pregnancy when she had exhausted her regular store of questions. He had expected her to raise the question of his getting married, but she didn't.

"Tell me about the professor, Mama," he said one morning.

It was two days before Halloween. From the kitchen, his eyes fixed on his mother's urns on the patio. They were weather-beaten and chipped. At the edge of the lawn, cherry blossom trees lined the tiny backyard. Their leaves were turning brittle and falling on the dried, yellow grass. Nizar hadn't seen any sign of life—rabbit or bird—venture close to the sliding doors for weeks.

For a moment, Nizar wondered if he'd uttered anything, but a long silence on the other end of the line confirmed he had.

"What do you want to know?" his mother asked. Her tone of voice did not change, though her volume slightly dropped.

In a way, Nizar had expected her to be undaunted—she was a woman who'd never shrunken under a man's heavy love for her, who'd left her children for hours in front of a television set with bowls of cereal, to be with her lover. In another way, it was profoundly unsettling that she could easily invite him through a portal to a woman's intimacy and passion—far beyond what his mother should possess in his then child-young eyes. He still couldn't understand the magnetic pull the other man had on his mother, drawing her away from their family for over a decade.

"Why didn't you marry him?" Nizar's voice sounded strange and hollow.

"He couldn't afford it when we met," she said. "My father—Seedo Ibrahim—liked him very much, but couldn't consent to a marriage until he could support me." His mother spoke like it was a secret she was finally relieved to surrender, to have someone else hold and appreciate its magnificent weight. "I was young and in love. I thought he'd come for me someday. I was the fool in the end—never your father. When you love another honestly as your father did, you can never be foolish."

"Okay," Nizar said. He was glad he could not see her face because he knew it would be easier to forgive her then.

"Okay, habibi."

"Do you want to talk to Baba?"

"Of course," she said.

His father was in the family room watching the Turkish soap operas from a satellite broadcast. In his lap was a half-eaten banana on a paper napkin Nizar had spread for him.

"Baba, Mama wants to talk to you." He handed his father the cordless phone and sat next to him on the couch.

"Suhad?" His father sat up straighter and happily chirped into the mouthpiece. "It's getting colder here. Yes—I've been wearing sweaters to the store."

Nizar patted his father's thigh, hearing the joy but not the actual words. After a few more moments, he left his parents alone to talk.

* * *

On Halloween, Nizar gave his father a bowl of candy for trick-o-treaters. When teenage boys walked in, Joey, the part-time security guard, instructed them to remove their masks and deposit their loot bags—dirty pillowcases and Hefty garbage bags—at the door.

"I can see why you need those masks—hiding ugly!" Joey's laugh was loud and barreling.

The boys just rolled their eyes and headed for a glass refrigerator filled with soft drinks and water bottles. One of them pulled out cans of Red Bull and handed them to each of his companions.

"The candy ain't enough to keep you wired?" Nizar asked the young leader who was peeling a ten-dollar bill from a wad in his jacket pocket.

"Man, just gimme my change," the leader said.

"Take some candy," Nizar's father said to the boys, extending them a fistful of cherry Jolly Ranchers as they passed.

When the bowl was empty, Nizar's father placed it on the counter in front of Nizar. "Your mother ate most of the candy you brought home—do you remember that? She liked the ones wrapped in orange and black that you kids immediately separated from the rest. What were they called?"

Nizar opened another bag of Jolly Ranchers and poured it into the bowl. "I never knew what those were called."

"'Mary Jane Kisses,'" Joey called out. He drank a Coca Cola Nizar's father offered him every shift and gestured with it when he spoke. His brown skin was like shiny new dates. "'Mary Jane Peanut Butter Kisses.'"

"No shit?" Nizar said. He couldn't remember ever tasting them. "Baba?" He touched his father's arm, which was sprawled across the counter. "What's wrong?"

His father's face was pale and perspiration dotted his forehead. "I'm fine, fine. Quit your nagging," he told Nizar.

Nizar began his evening ritual of bundling twenty-dollar bills from each cash register drawer. "Are you hungry? I'll order something from Jack's."

His father shook his head and looked at Nizar. His face was serene and unclouded. In that moment, he was Nizar's father as he had been before the disease.

Nizar felt a lump in his throat. He wanted to say something quickly before his father disappeared back into the dark forest of his mind from which he had seemed to temporarily escape. And his father appeared to be searching for words. After a few moments, his father only patted Nizar's face.

Nizar stood with rolls of paper bills. He, too, was unable to summon any words, feeling as feeble as his father.

His father trudged down an aisle, toward the back of the store.

"Do you need help in the washroom, Baba?" Nizar asked. His father didn't answer.

After Nizar closed out the second cash register drawer, he and the store clerks heard a screech of tires then a heavy thud. A woman was screaming.

"Goddamn cars! Can't slow down for shit," Joey said, shaking his head.

"Call 9-1-1," Nizar said. He knocked on the washroom door and it swung open. "Baba?" He headed to the front of the store. "Henry," he called to a clerk. "Did you see my father?" Before Henry could answer, Nizar rushed outside.

Parents stood with hands clamped over their mouths, beside them their children in skeleton costumes and clown faces, fidgeting and peering into the street. Nizar worried the sight of an injured child would upset his father. "Baba?" He searched the crowd.

"Is he your father?" a woman asked. She was wearing a witch's hat and ordinary clothes. He just walked right into the street without stopping." The other women and men nodded and sucked their teeth.

Nizar first glimpsed his father's arm, grotesquely twisted out and away from the rest of his body. He pushed through more people and pulled a man away who was squatting down next to his father. The old man was on his stomach, and his head was turned to the right, a dark pool of blood seeping from it. The exposed side of his face did not contain a single scratch. His eyelids were half-open as though he'd been struck while waking up from a nap.

Nizar ripped off his clerk apron and tried to stem the flow, but the blood soaked through until there was no more fabric to absorb it, drenching Nizar's hands next. He carefully turned his father over and cradled his head in his lap. His fingers brushed against shattered skull bone piercing his father's scalp.

Nizar shrieked for help, but his voice was distant from him, like an echo in a thick fog. A macabre carnival of masked and painted faces watched him from the sidewalk.

The Great Chicago Fire

His right eyelid was like an apricot pulp forgotten in the sun too long, its once inviting color long faded. My parents wanted me to call him *khalo*, but *khalo* meant *uncle*, and *uncle* was familiar, yet this man wasn't familiar to me at all. Though he and my mother shared the same thick, ebony hair, my uncle's was shorn of any volume and nearly all gray. He was younger than my mother. The only gray in her hair crept evenly from the part line of her crown and would soon disappear after her next salon appointment.

It was hard to imagine my uncle Ziyad as a young boy, running after my mother, wanting to be included in her games with the other neighborhood kids in Nur Shams, the refugee camp where they were born. Twenty years ago, my mother had fled the sewage stench and corrugated tin roofs when she married my father, a thriving liquor storeowner in Roseland. He would build her a house far from that violent neighborhood in a suburb full of other Arabs who'd never have to go back to curfews and black-outs, and days of eating stale khubuz because you couldn't get to the baker for fresh bread when the Israelis put up roadblocks, dissecting the camp like vital organs, in search of militants. These details emerged from my mother's former life when she chastised my laziness or discovered I'd thrown away half a slice of frozen pizza in the kitchen trash bin, and such stories dampened my adolescent defiance and guilt tingled my spine.

When my uncle was released from Israel's Nafha prison, he lived a while in Portugal with some distant relatives whose grandparents had fled the 1948 occupation and had remained there for three generations. When my parents finally arranged for my uncle's visit to the U.S., my mother cried for a whole week as she cooked and cleaned our split-level house, ordering me to clean out the basement and help her tidy our spare bedroom, a space which had housed all of my childhood memorabilia in black-markered storage boxes.

"I'm sure you'll find the best arrabi food here," my father assured my uncle. "Though still not as delicious as your sister's cooking." He winked at my mother and playfully mussed my hair until I flicked his hand away.

"Baba, quit it!" I told him, sullen about having to spend another evening home as guests continued filing in and out of our house to welcome my uncle Ziyad and stake a weekend for a grand dinner at their homes in honor of his long overdue arrival.

"I doubt anything made from my sister's hands is not the best quality," my uncle Ziyad said, his voice soft and his words unhurried.

"Tomorrow we'll drive into the city, show you all the extraordinary sights Chicago has to offer," my father proudly announced, sounding as though he'd been born in this country and in the very city when he'd been here merely five years before he brought my mother from overseas to join him, leaving behind my grandparents and other uncles and aunts and first and second cousins I was not likely to ever meet.

Tonight at our house more men arrived in pressed slacks and heavy sweaters, and some wore crisp white dress shirts. Khalo Ziyad appeared smaller than them, lodged between two heavy-set men. He was the only one wearing jeans, a pair with frayed bottoms and tinged yellow, the same pair he'd been wearing the day he arrived at O'Hare International Airport and which my mother had immediately washed for him. She'd set out a pair of my father's flannel pants that he'd lounge in on weekends when he wasn't at his liquor store. My father had given my uncle Ziyad a sports jacket, hoping he'd look more presentable, but the jacket swallowed up his torso and thin arms and he looked like a boy wearing his father's suit for a pageant at school.

In our kitchen, the women busied themselves with plates of tangy spinach ikras and baklawa, layers of golden pastry soaked in syrup. They prepared several pots of coffee—American and the thick Turkish kind that lined the bottom of my mother's fancy demitasse cups with blackish-brown sediment. They talked over and past each other, pinching each other's arms in affectionate replies, and giggling like young girls again. Their voices rose in crescendos, yet never seemed to descend. I felt a warmth in their unfettered exuberance as I wiped down the countertop until I realized how futile it was while the women continued to serve coffee, then tea, honey-colored liquid splattering onto the speckled granite.

I sat on a kitchen stool and watched the turning leaves cling to the branches of a maple tree in our yard. A few snapped away and floated to the damp ground. In a few weeks, the fallen leaves would be buried in the first layer of snow. I wondered if my uncle Ziyad had ever seen snow and how he'd need a decent coat if he were to brave his first Illinois winter. I stared at my uncle Ziyad's profile, his good eye to me until he turned and caught me staring. He gave me a small nod and turned back to the men's whooping conversations.

* * *

My father began his amateur tour guide of the city at the Midway Plaisance. It was a pretty boring stretch of autumn-browned lawn. The dilapidated houses with broken sidewalks kept my father from actually stopping the car and letting my uncle Ziyad take a walk down the Midway where side-shows and vendors had set up during the 1893 World's Fair.

"And the Arabs stayed," my father was telling him. "They worked hard and lived the American Dream. Al hilm al amarkani," he added for effect.

I noticed my mother didn't say much when my father dominated the conversation. She let her brother sit in front and she took my hand in her lap and caressed it as she stared out the window of the car, nodding to no one in particular.

We drove north on Lake Shore Drive and Lake Michigan looked gray and lovely. A few sailboats bobbed in the distance and joggers in shorts and earmuffs ran in both directions, alongside the lake.

"We'll save Navy Pier for this evening," my father said. "Ziyad will get the fireworks tonight." He reached over and patted his brother-in-law's shoulder.

My uncle Ziyad didn't say much, only turning to look in the direction my father pointed. I couldn't tell if he was completely unimpressed or overwhelmed. I'd discovered he was like a break-wall against which the waves of Lake Michigan crashed but never penetrated. It made me wonder what he thought of us, our house in a neat suburb, the city, and everything that made us distinctly separate and safe from whatever he had experienced in that prison.

* * *

My father finally parked the car off Rush Street and we walked east to Michigan Avenue. We walked past women in high-heeled boots and dark sunglasses, their necks lost in layers of woolen scarves. It was easy to distinguish the natives from the tourists: European men and women, fit and tanned, their children wearing designer sneakers and wind-breakers; Asians in large groups of families and friends, following a leader with a poised camera;

and finally, the suburbanites like us who reveled in the city and glad that we could easily leave all its noise, glass-paneled skyscrapers, and homeless folks, retreating to our quiet and neatly manufactured neighborhoods.

I tried imagining it through my uncle Ziyad's eyes. Was he impressed? My mother locked one arm through my father's and they walked ahead of me and my uncle. When we arrived at the old Water Tower, my father began his effusive tour-guide script again.

"Imagine, Ziyad, that only one-hundred and forty years ago, this was one of a few buildings left standing after the Big Chicago Fire," my father declared.

"The Great Chicago Fire, Baba," I corrected him. "Not Big."

"Yes, yes. The Great Chicago Fire," he said. "Anyhow, the point is, that Chicagoans didn't let anything stop their progress in the modern world."

For the first time, my uncle Ziyad's interest appeared piqued. "Who started the fire?" he asked. His pulpy eyelid slightly lifted to reveal an undamaged pupil.

My father smiled widely, encouraged by his brother-in-law's inquiry. "It's a funny story," he began. "A baqarra—a cow—had knocked over a lamp in a barn."

"Baba, that was never proven," I interjected. I'm not sure what compelled me to challenge my father, but I continued, drawing from a history lesson last year when my class was studying Chicago architecture in AP Art. "In fact, that woman was publicly exonerated of any wrong-doing." And suddenly, other details surfaced like I'd tapped a spring in my brain. "She and other Irish people were harassed for a long time when it wasn't even her fault. Ms. Vernon—my art teacher—said it was a terrible time for Irish immigrants in this city."

My uncle Ziyad seemed to be listening intently. He wanted to know all that the fire had destroyed, how many people had perished and had been displaced. He wasn't interested in how the city was rebuilt or its progress since the blaze. But my father continued to steer the conversation back to the wonder of structures like the Water Tower and what came after the fire—a newly imagined city with the world's first skyscrapers—all of the tales of ambition and vision that real tour-guides extolled upon their eager-eyed patrons who visited Chicago for the first time.

And yet my uncle Ziyad had stopped listening again. He walked ahead of us and stared at the bronze plaque mounted on one side of the pale bricks of the Water Tower, commemorating its architect. His shoulders were stooped and he did not blend in with the other tourists who huddled around the plaque and snapped photos.

And I finally understood. Those houses were wooden, turned to ash, no traces left so that the city could begin again, improvise, go in a new a direction. The houses in my mother and uncle's refugee camp that the Israeli's fired rockets into were made of cinderblock that barely disintegrated in fire, only gutting its interiors, leaving behind ghastly skeletons with thick charred wires of what had once been.

Widow

The only arrabi Aisha had ever loved and married was shot five times in the chest at a liquor store he owned with two brothers on 47th and Halsted Street. Chicago newscasters said crimes went up when temperatures went up. It wasn't one of the hottest summers in 2009; the summer Aisha's husband was killed had only seven ninety-degree days.

I'd driven by that liquor store once to avoid highway traffic on I-94. Storefronts were converted into neighborhood ministries and fast-food joints had glumly faded signs and windows with steel bars. The bleakness hung in the air like the stench of dirty diapers tossed into empty parking lots.

After the shooting, Aisha stopped eating. Stopped talking and dressing up nice. A year passed and she showed up at Nahla's bridal shower at the rec center in Orland Park. She was a fucking ghost. But she was still pretty like the porcelain dolls my mother collected. Those dolls had looked even whiter against our olive-skinned hands when my sisters and I were allowed to hold them when we were kids.

And Aisha looked sad. Hollow eyes staring right through you. She walked in with a small wrapped box that seemed too heavy for her to carry. She looked like she didn't know what to do with the present even though the table with all the shower gifts was only a few feet away, past the round tables of women all turning to look at her.

"Ya haram!" my oldest sister Jinan said every time we talked about Aisha in our mother's kitchen. "To lose your husband before your first anniversary! She was the finest girl in our whole school. Could have had any guy." And Jinan would shake her head. Jinan didn't finish high school and got married when she was seventeen years old. She thought she couldn't do better than Shadi—a real prick who liked to correct her Arabic in front of his friends and flicked crusty flakes from his nostrils when he was talking to you. She figured with her bad acne and being as short as a middle school kid, he was a catch. Jinan was damned nice, though, and had a sweet singsong voice. Even angry, she still sounded like Celine Dion or somebody.

"No excuse to go after married men," Hiyam, my other sister said, pointing at Jinan with her cigarette. "No fucking excuse for that. I don't care how goddamn tragic her loss is." Hiyam adjusted her bra strap with her free fingers then pulled back her thick brown hair over her shoulder. It was hard to like Hiyam—even as my sister—when she already had an advantage over most girls with her full lips and perfect nose. Like Jinan, she was short but Hiyam had great boobs and an ass that was big enough to be sexy and not hoochie. She was pretty, but she was mean, too. It baffled me that being nice didn't always follow good looks. And it couldn't have been easy for poor Jinan. At least I was tall and slender, like my father.

"I've been hearing all kinds of shit about Aisha," Hiyam said. She stubbed out her cigarette in a Niagara Falls souvenir ashtray.

"Watch your mouth," my mother scolded her from the stove. She was dunking cabbage leaves in a steep pot of boiling water.

People had started calling Aisha a *sharmoota*—a whore. It wasn't to be mean. You sleep with other women's husbands and the label sticks like gum to the bottom of your shoe.

At that shower, the bride-to-be had given her a limp hug, not wanting to touch her too hard or too long like Aisha had some kind of disease the bride was afraid of catching before her wedding day. I couldn't help but feel sorry for Aisha. But, I kept it to myself. My sister Hiyam wasn't as kind.

Across the kitchen table, Hiyam inhaled deeply and let the smoke exit her nostrils. I couldn't stand it when women did that when they smoked. It's so unattractive—unladylike. But, I kept quiet.

"If you mess around with married men, you're izballah," Hiyam said. "Downright trash."

"Hiyam!" My mother hissed. "Watch your mouth."

It went around that Aisha was sleeping with Muneer, a guy we grew up with on the Southside. I used to walk to Nightingale Elementary School with him along with a small flock of neighborhood kids. We were less likely to get bullied by the white kids who saw a bunch of dark-skinned "camel-jockeys" scuttling down the block, and not one or two helpless stragglers.

Once, in second grade, I peed in my pants right before the dismissal bell—thought I could hold it until I got home. Held it like that all the time when I was a kid. And no matter how much my mother threatened to burn my butt with filfil—a hot pepper—I still kept it up. If my sisters or me talked nasty, she threatened filfil in our mouths—other infractions were a hot pepper up the butt, which I sometimes wished she'd do to Hiyam. But, my mother always scared us just enough with words.

On that day, I stood up from my desk and my jeans were dark with warm urine between my legs. Everyone in the group believed me when I told them a dumb boy spilled his soda on me. Except for Muneer.

"Liar," he said when we reached the corner of our block. "Teacher wouldn't let him drink pop in class."

"I know, stupid," I said. "He opened it when she wasn't looking and when she walked down our row he tried to hide it under his desk and my desk is right next to his and he spilled it on me." I explained it just like that—all in one breath the way kids do under pressure.

"You peed, you liar. Mariam peed in her pants!" He shrieked that the rest of the way home.

People said this same Muneer screwed Aisha right there in the back office at his used car lot in Oak Lawn. No doubt he was still an asshole, and the last I'd seen him he'd grown real hairy, too.

We were smoking shisha one night when my friend Ruba told me what her husband told her. We passed the tube of the hookah back and forth and she told me Aisha had come out of his office looking like she did nothing more than sign a contract to buy a Camry from Muneer.

"Who'd want to screw him," I said to Ruba.

"That's not the point," she said, annoyed.

"I'm just saying. He's got back hair creeping out of his shirt like a ferret."

"You're disgusting, Mariam," Ruba said, wiping a trickle of saliva off the mouthpiece of the tube before passing it to me.

People like my sister Hiyam said there were others, that married men would line up to fuck arabiyat like Aisha who weren't a virgin. To these jerks, divorced women were like getting the milk for free. They might take care of a woman's rent or buy her a Louis Vuitton handbag—no way did they ever actually leave their wives. But, Aisha didn't need money. Her husband had cut a life insurance policy that people said she had no idea he'd had. Anyway, she was set even though his brothers tried to claim half of it. She didn't need a sugar daddy or any arrabi scumbag.

Before Muneer, some said she was messing around with Amjad, a real estate broker whose face was plastered on billboards and bus stop benches near the mosque in Bridgeview.

"How's Azzam?" Ruba asked me, taking another hit off the tube. The water base gurgled with pleasure as she inhaled.

"He's fine," I told her. Whenever another person mentioned his name, I got a funny feeling under my chin like someone tickling me with a feather or something. I tried to keep my eyes even with Ruba, tried not to avert them when we talked about Azzam. But, he was the kind of guy who did that to a girl, who made her feel all tingling and warm, and not in a sexual way—or not *only* in that way—but in a way that made you anxious to see him and already anxious to part company even before you had seen him.

"He make a move yet?" Ruba asked.

"We're just friends," I said. "How many times have I told you that?"

"Not enough to believe you," Ruba said. She wiped the mouthpiece across her sleeve and passed me the tube.

I ignored her, glad to use my mouth for smoking and not talking.

* * *

At the bridal shower, the same women who'd been gossiping as soon as she walked in swarmed around Aisha, all talking at once and inviting her to sit with them. Goddamn hypocrites. As long as she stayed away from their sons and sons-in-law they could drench Aisha in their two-faced sympathy. She spent about ten minutes kissing each woman on both cheeks, letting them hold her thin wrists as they spouted lame condolences.

"Allah yarhamo," they all said. She just smiled and nodded her head. Then she cut a path through the horde of women and headed straight for my table. Just left those cows standing there like a bunch of dumb-asses.

"Can I sit here?" she asked.

"Sure," I said. Both of my sisters—no longer on the prowl for husbands—had made excuses not to attend so I was alone.

The young girls at my table were fidgety and bored, waiting for the deejay to start playing so they could get up and shake their asses. They were slumped over their cell phones or listening to each other with lazy elbows propped on the plastic-covered table. When a girl entered the rec room, they quickly straightened up and leaned against the back of their rental chairs, trying to check out her outfit without looking obvious. Then they'd whisper and roll their eyes, giggling sometimes. If they approved, they'd give each other a *not-bad* lift of their eyebrows.

Close up, Aisha was prettier than any woman I had seen and in Orland Park there were plenty of Palestinian princesses who could be the next Miss America if their parents let them wear a bikini on public T.V.

Difference was Aisha was natural. Smooth-skinned and pale like a white peach. Her lips were full and red-stained, but she wasn't wearing any lipstick or gloss. All natural. When she looked me full in the face I caught a glint of green in her brown eyes. Not even a hint of mascara, and her lids were heavy—the kind that my sister Jinan calls sensuous. *Men love eyelids like that*, she'd told me.

I felt awkward sitting across from Aisha because she was so pretty and I could have been part of the fucking wallpaper in that rec room. And I knew we were both the same age, but she seemed older than twenty-four, like she'd been through a war. And damn if I knew what to say to her about her dead husband. Maybe it's too late after a year to offer your sympathy. Too late to tell her I couldn't imagine losing anyone close especially one who'd seen me naked and still loved me. I decided to let it go. Let her talk first.

Aisha didn't utter a single word except to say *thanks* and *you're welcome* when the other girls passed saltshakers and packets of Sweet 'n Low across the table. You could hear everyone trying to talk louder and faster than each other, fighting to get their scraps of gossip in before they were beaten to the punch or outdone by even juicier news. Laughter rose like cackles. The noises got harder to separate the longer you sat there. Until the music started. The deejay Intisar finished assembling her turntable and played that stupid "Shik-Shak-Shok" song, and young girls screamed and jumped from their chairs to dance. Intisar was hired for most parties and gender-split weddings and showed up wearing a funky, animal print hijab on her head and yoga pants with PINK stitched across her ass. She cracked funny and nasty jokes in English about the bride's virginity and its expiration. The older women pretended they didn't understand.

Food was always damn good at these things. Only reason I ever showed up. My mom—a real pain in my ass—insists I show my face at these events like maybe I can snag a husband if his mother, sister, or cousin happens to see me and not totally count me out of the game. I could give a shit, really. I had long ago folded my cards. But, I guess I could play another hand if Azzam was back in the game, too.

He was the only arrabi I knew in college who read an entire book for enjoyment—and not just his pharmacy textbooks. Always memoirs, too. Like Bill Clinton's *My Life* and biographies on Gamal Abdel Nasser. We had a couple Gen Ed classes together at UIC, and started hanging out at the Commons. He was too serious for those other clowns who spent most of their time flirting with any arabiyat in push-up bras.

When we were hungry we went to a dive called Couscous off Taylor Street for baba ghanoush. I loved the smoked eggplant dip—could eat it all day long. Azzam ordered falafel and hummus. I didn't care what the girls said about the two of us eating together or when we studied in the library. It didn't matter anyway. In the end, Azzam was just not feeling it for me. And I pretended being friends was enough.

At the shower, the buffet line had dwindled and I grabbed a foam plate, ready to scoop a little bit of everything onto it until it threatened to split in half. With all the glitzy dresses and decked out nails, you'd think the bride's mother might have sprung for some fucking Chinet plates or something. *Fabulously cheap*, my friend Ruba would've called it.

At least they didn't skimp on the menu. Waraq dawali steamed from a giant platter; the shiny rolled grape leaves looked like green logs stacked for the winter. Fried chicken, rice and beef, and ikras—those spinach pies spiced with tangy purple summac. And mostaccioli. Never failed. A Middle Eastern feast topped with goddamn mostaccioli. But I'm not complaining.

As soon as the music started, my table emptied and it was just Aisha and me watching the other women clap their hands and the younger ones sway their hips to the beat of the tablah and tambourines from other popular belly-dancing tracks the deejay spun. As soon as the male waiters were gone, some of the women took off their hijab and whipped open their abayas, showing off tight, sleeveless dresses. Victoria's Secret boobs were all over the place.

None of these girls gave two shits about playing shower games, like making the bride eat a marshmallow each time she gave a wrong answer about her soon-to-be husband, until her cheeks puffed up like a chipmunk. And everyone figured the bride had registered for her gifts at Bed Bath And Beyond so it was a waste of time to open them while she faked sheer delight. These parties were for showing off, meeting your future mother-in-law, and churning out new rumors. I'd been to the shower of a white girl I knew from the temp agency where I worked, and when I asked where the deejay was she couldn't stop laughing. One of her bridesmaids gave me a raffle ticket and we filled out silly game sheets for prizes. I won a tiny electric crockpot and potpourri. One of the best showers I'd ever attended—except for the food.

On the dance floor, the bride was in the center, swaying her hips, her arms fluttering above her head. Her sisters and close friends linked hands and danced around her. Aisha was still nibbling her food, pushing parts of it in opposite directions than shoveling them back to the center with her plastic fork. A woman with a big mole beneath one of her eyes was talking her ear off. As soon as our table cleared out, the woman had practically run over to us—waddled is more like it, her heavy body fighting hard to maintain a core of balance. Plopped in a chair beside Aisha, with most of her ass falling out of her seat.

Aisha didn't even look at the woman, just nodded and stared ahead, sometimes glancing at me, like she was working out a problem in her head. I'd give her a small smile when our eyes met and before I could help it, I rolled my eyes in sympathy and did a yapping gesture with my hand as Mole Woman rattled on about her son's wife not being able to get pregnant, or some private shit.

"Aib! Shame on you"! the woman snapped at me. "You think I'm blind! You have no manners!"

I was so startled that I think I jumped. Felt dumb as shit. I tried to make amends quickly, but Mole Woman just heaved herself up, red face and all, and waddled away.

"What the fuck," I said.

"Forget about her. She's a nosey-body," Aisha said.

I picked up my glass of water and took a long sip to hide my flushed face. How fucking old was I anyhow? Yelling at me like I was two. Giant penguin-bitch.

I must have uttered that last bit out loud because Aisha was laughing. When I looked over at her, her peachy complexion turned rosier as her laughter gained momentum. She wiped tears away from the rims of her lower eyelids. Did it delicately with the knuckle of her finger. People who cry when they laugh always amuse me. Seems honest, sincere.

"These women are driving me nuts," she said. "I didn't even want to come, but my mother thinks I'll have fun." She sipped her Diet Coke straight from the can, drumming her fingers on the table in time to the beat of the music.

"My mom always makes me come to these things," I commiserated. And then we laughed. Two twenty-something's still trying to please their mothers. "At least the food's good," I said.

"Elhamdulillah," she said. "Thank God for that." She scanned the room, still drumming her fingers. "I forgot how ridiculous these parties are."

"It's like a fucking pageant," I said. She laughed again. We watched tanned dancing girls glisten with perspiration like rotisserie chickens.

For the rest of the night, I'd forgotten about the stories of her and that scumbag Muneer at his car lot. I stole glimpses of her delicate profile while we observed the party, and it was easier to picture her sitting on a couch, her husband's head in her lap. With an ivory hand, soft and translucent, she was tenderly stroking his thick hair while he told her about a long day at his liquor store.

* * *

"So I heard you two are like b-f-fs now," my sister Hiyam said when I walked into the kitchen the next morning, still rubbing the crusty sleepiness out of my eyes. She was already sitting at the table at the ass-crack of dawn with her two little brats. Call me bitchy for saying so about my twin nephews, but, wallah, they're monsters. Always breaking my stuff and clogging up the toilet with their toys.

"We sat at the same table," I said. "She's actually nice." Hiyam sucked her teeth, which I hated just as much as the way she exhaled smoke through her nostrils.

I craned my neck into the hallway. "Rami! Sam! Get off my bed!" I could hear their muffled giggles then two thumps on the floor.

"She's nice, huh?" Hiyam said. She was fingering the rim of her coffee mug. "Well, I guess you have nothing to worry about."

"What do you mean?" But, I knew what she meant and let her say it anyway.

"You don't have a man, so you're safe," she said. Hiyam had been a bully since we were kids. She'd make me do horrible things like pick up dog shit or touch a dead bee so I'd be allowed to play with her and Jinan, who always came to my rescue.

"Bas, ya Hiyam," my mother said. "Enough!" She was rinsing hard-boiled eggs in cold water at the sink.

"You're a bitch," I said, heading back to bed.

"Mariam, come have breakfast!" my mother called after me.

I felt tired again like I was getting ready for bed when I actually had to hurry to get ready for work. But I just lay there in my bed, staring at the ceiling fan, my arm arched above my head on the pillow. I listened to the garbage truck rumbling down the street, releasing a swoosh each time it braked. As it scooped the trash, the compactor made a sound like crushing metal.

The sunlight warmed my comforter. My mother came in every morning and opened the curtains to wake me up. Never worked though. I could sleep in broad daylight no matter where I was. I figured stuff like that made a person easy-going. A person like that could handle most situations.

I turned away from my window and pulled the sheet over my head. From the kitchen, my mother was scolding the twins. She finally shooed them into the backyard.

I was more than a little irritated by Hiyam. What did she think? I'd end up an old maid? A spinster? How fucking old-fashioned. Look at *her* goddamn husband. You can't take my lame-ass brother-in-law anywhere without him getting obnoxious, especially when he talked politics. He was like the Arab version of Glenn Beck.

And, look at Aisha. A twenty-four year old widow. Could anything be worse than that?

I lifted the cotton sheet away from my face. Shit. Now Azzam was floating around in my head. I'd become really good at quickly snuffing out any image of him that popped up. It was easy, like crushing a cigarette in an ashtray until every bright ember no longer burned.

During our sophomore year in college, Azzam gave me a copy of *The Other Wes Moore.*

"For eid," he'd said.

Ramadan was finally over and we could have coffee and smoke cigarettes between classes again. I hadn't gotten him anything to celebrate the holiday, but he looked like he hadn't expected a gift from me and would have been embarrassed if I'd handed him something.

"It's a crazy true story," he explained, taking it back and rifling to the sections containing photographs. "These two black guys grew up in the same rough neighborhood, had the same name. One made it out. The other's serving a life sentence for murder."

"Nice spoiler alert," I joked. "Thanks for ruining it."

"No, no—you'll love it," he said. "I figure you're a psych major. You might find it interesting." He handed it back to me and gave me an awkward smile. Then I felt like an asshole, like I'd wrecked the moment.

I read the book in less than a week just so I could discuss it with Azzam. He seemed pleased by my responses to specific parts.

Now the book was on my shelf, crammed between hardcover textbooks and my old Stephen King novels. Not even nine o'clock in the morning and I was already feeling fucking pathetic under my bed sheet. Only a scalding hot shower and two cups of coffee later was I better.

The next time I saw Aisha was at a hinna for my second cousin Taghreed whose first words at birth were "must find a husband." She wasn't exactly intolerable, but she made things very difficult for me when our families gathered. Her mother, Aunty Anaam, was my father's cousin. She had one of those faces that looked like it had been stretched out and had lost its elasticity so her skin hung loosely in thin folds. She was pretty nice, though. She'd give me a sympathetic look, like she was embarrassed that her daughter was getting hitched when a loser like me was still wading in the singles' pool.

The women placed a large platter of moist homemade hinna decorated with carnations on Taghreed's head. She gripped it with both hands and danced around while everyone clapped. Seemed silly, but it was an old *fellahi* tradition, and I actually liked this part. After the last ululation, young girls passed out plastic cups of the dye to every table. It smelled like wet tea leaves and mud. I looked around and most of the women used their fingers to scoop out the stuff. On the back of their hands, they traced their lovers' initials inside a sloppy heart that looked like it was drawn by a first-grader. You had to wait at least ten minutes until the hinna dried and flaked off, and what remained was a burnt-orange image. After a week, it turned into a shadow of something once exciting, like most things that don't last.

A professional artist hired by the groom's family did Taghreed's designs. When she appeared on the dance floor again, her hands were covered entirely by an elaborate network of flower stems and petals. It looked real pretty. Taghreed's face was tense when someone danced too close to her, and she moved her arms like a tyrannosaurus rex so no one would smudge the still-wet hinna.

When Aisha arrived, she walked past tables of the same gossiping women. She was with her mother this time and a boy who must have been her little brother. Threw me a slight nod and smiled. I waved back, then felt foolish like it was too big a gesture in return. I was secretly disappointed she didn't sit with me.

Her mother embraced other guests with a stiff back, her chin jutting up into the air when she quickly kissed someone on both cheeks. She wore her daughter's misfortune like a boa constrictor around her neck. You couldn't blame the woman, really. Old school arabiyat could handle most calamities, but their daughter's reputation was like one of those *Star Wars* collector figures wrapped in cellophane. As soon as you peeled the plastic off of the box, you've trashed Princess Leia. Aisha's good name—her sim'aa—had been busted out of its box as soon as she let those douche-bags lay their hands on her.

If we had become friends, I could have told her I understood why she did it. Maybe she still smelled her dead husband every time she hung clothes in their bedroom closet—that spicy cologne might still be lingering in places, jolting her for a minute before she caught her breath. Or maybe she was tired of shredding junk mail addressed to him. Tired of looking at a bed that suddenly appeared wider when she sank into it, feeling like she was afloat every night, without his warm body to anchor her.

I could have told her I knew how desperately we needed to erase every last trace of someone, that fucking Muneer might have stripped away the memory of her husband's fingers caressing her back. I could understand all that.

* * *

The wedding season was over by late August. I was trying to figure out what the hell I wanted to do with my life. The psychology degree I earned two years ago was useless. I could either go to grad school or get certification to teach. Until I was motivated enough to make a decision, I stayed working at the temp agency, filing paperwork for clients who were in worse shape than me.

"Did you hear about Aisha?" Hiyam said one evening after I got home. My sister's eyes were liquid with giddiness. I couldn't ignore her, so I said, "What?"

"She's pregnant," Hiyam said. She took a few long drags of her cigarette then stubbed it out. "That sharmoota is pregnant."

"She's not a sharmoota," I said. Regretted it immediately, though, because Hiyam pounced like a cougar.

"How can you defend her? She's been sleeping with a married man with three kids. You're such a habla. A total dumb-ass."

"Hiyam, bas," my mother said. "Enough already." She was standing as usual at the stove with a large fork, her back turned to us. She was frying cauliflower for maklooba, the upside-down rice dish. When we were kids, we'd wait for my mother to carefully flip the big pot of lamb meat, cauliflower, potato slices, and rice onto a huge silver platter. For a few seconds, it was like a cake sprung from a tin mold. We'd try to get through three verses of

'Happy Birthday' before all the vegetables, meat and rice toppled.

Hiyam tapped a fresh cigarette out of her box of Marlboro Lights and lit it, the whole time staring me down. For a second, I thought the flame would lick the tip of her nose. Hoped, to tell you the truth.

I left her and my mother to consider what Muneer's wife must be thinking. I ran warm water in the bathroom sink and lathered up the soap bar. I gently massaged my face, rubbing away eye shadow and blush. I don't know why, but I was sad all of a sudden. I felt a ripple in my stomach, like a puddle of water disturbed by a breeze. I rinsed my face and went to my bedroom to change.

Before we graduated, Azzam told me that he was going to hold off getting married as long as he could. Damn though if his mother hadn't already assembled a line of girls. Like fucking cheerleaders poised to jump, flip and win him over.

I knew a few of them—one I really couldn't stand. She worked at Best Buy and had boobs like parking cones. 1940s pin-up boobs. When she turned, her ass was flat—my only consolation—but she had enough highlighted blonde hair to distract you from that deficit. She wore plum lip-liner and a pink shade of lipstick. Drives me crazy when girls do that. I read in *Marie Claire* that you're supposed to fill in lipstick *first* then a liner with a *matching* color—not a shade ten times lighter. So fucking tacky.

The other female contenders were not so bad. I was surprised, though, when he mentioned Hanan. We'd gone to the same high school. She had a lazy eye that she tried to hide with long sweeping side-bangs. Didn't think his mother would allow a flaw like that. But, Hanan came from a big-money family originally from Jerusalem, and Azzam's mother was a peasant, trying to lure daughters of city clans to marry every one of her sons. Hanan was sweet. That lazy eye made her seem more real.

Azzam always laughed when I imitated his mother. *'This girl ferry nice and britty—hilwa wa na'ima, ya habibi. She make many sons for you, inshallah.'*

He'd said, "Hell no. I want to travel first before marriage and all that shit."

"Me, too," I said. We both knew it would never happen for me, but Azzam smiled politely and squeezed the back of my neck. My parents were already skittish about my sisters and me going to college even though each one of us attended in-state and had commuted for God's sake. No arabiyat ever dormed unless they were Egyptian or Lebanese—or had parents who were super-progressive Palestinians. We were jealous of those girls.

I liked imagining Azzam and me somewhere like Italy where we'd visit cathedrals—we wouldn't tell any of our families about that—and we'd laugh and complain when we had to pay to use the public toilets. We would have read about all the un-touristy places beforehand, and discover a gem like Certaldo, a town in Tuscany. And we'd stay at a monastery where Benedictine monks lived during the fourteenth century and had welcomed pilgrims passing through the town. I liked to imagine us sleeping where medieval men and women rested on their way to their holy destination.

Azzam took one trip to Costa Rica after graduation. He posted pics almost every day on Facebook when he was there. It was so like him to expose the poverty of places alongside images of him standing innocently between two gorgeous native girls. He got a hundred likes and comments on his status. I was worried he would overlook my funny messages. But he never missed one. Always commented with more than a stupid emoticon.

He rarely changed his profile pic, replacing it only with a Palestinian flag in solidarity when some new violence overseas happened, or some other symbol denouncing U.S. foreign policy or the wealth gap.

I loved his pic. To a stranger, it looked goofy. The kind of pic most of us would never post because we're too fucking vain, but Azzam didn't care. It was probably the only one he ever took of himself. You could tell he didn't know exactly what he was doing, holding his camera high, aiming it at that awkward angle. He looked like he was on the brink of smiling but the shutter just missed it by a millisecond. His eyes were slightly squinting like he'd been counting down, bracing for the flash.

Almost seven months after his trip to Costa Rica, he uploaded a new profile pic. He was standing behind a girl I didn't recognize, scooping her inside his embrace. This time the camera captured his smile. My stomach felt tight, like I just swallowed something without chewing it first.

The next day I talked to my friend Ruba. "Guys are so full of shit," she said.

"Right," I said.

Azzam had sworn off romance to find himself, and look at him now. He was another idiot with a heart symbol for his relationship status on fucking Facebook.

"I told you," Ruba said. "Even the smart ones need to get laid."

A part of me wished I had slept with Azzam and then maybe—even if it was just for a flash—he would have seen me when he was with his girl. And even if I hadn't been the best sex of his life if we had actually done it, I bet he would have remembered the way I touched him—maybe on his shoulder, or maybe on the small of his back—and he would have remembered me.

In the end, I suppose I was glad. I mean who wants to wait around for someone, right? I guess that's why I didn't have much to say when we gathered around my mother's kitchen and Hiyam reported loud and bitchy that Aisha was getting married to some immigrant arrabi with a Ph.D. in third world economics. It was a few months after her baby-scandal had broke.

"Or some kind of global shit," Hiyam said.

"What about Muneer and the baby?" Jinan said. To me, she asked, "How do you like it? I added a little rosewater. Can you taste it?"

I took small scoops of her rice pudding from a glass bowl sprinkled with cinnamon. We were all eating from the same bowl. "It's really good," I told her, licking the back of my spoon. I pretended I wasn't interested in the talk—it was true—that Aisha was getting married again.

"Aw, shit! You didn't hear," Hiyam said. She made sure that my mother who'd gone into the basement to start a load of laundry was out of earshot. "Fucking got rid of it. Can you believe that shit?"

"Got rid of what?" Jinan asked distractedly. She was studying my face as I ate her rice pudding. I'd heard it, but Jinan thought it was her concoction that changed my expression.

"The baby," Hiyam said. "She got rid of it."

I stopped eating and Jinan and I looked at Hiyam. It seemed like a terrible thing to say over goddamn rice pudding.

Then Jinan looked over at me for a moment and said, "Well, at least she can start over."

My cheeks felt like they were pulsating and I hoped Hiyam hadn't noticed them reddening. I leaned over the table to sample some more of Jinan's rice pudding. I let the cool, custardy texture linger on my tongue, waiting for it to dissolve until all that was left were tender grains of rice, that wouldn't completely melt away. I finally swallowed.

"You're right," I said to Jinan. "Who wants to be a fucking widow for the rest of her life?"

My sister Hiyam didn't say anything after that. Took a long drag from her cigarette then stubbed it out.

Failed Treaties

Danny used to open the door and let me into his apartment at seven a.m. every Saturday. My mother would already be up, stooped over the kitchen table in her pale-blue nightdress, spreading tangy lebanah in a plate for my father before he left to open his grocery store. My baby sister Leena sucked on her chubby fist and squirmed in her highchair when I tickled her face. My mother blocked my way to the back door, holding a spoonful of yogurt in one hand and my chin in the other, sniffing my breath for traces of Colgate.

"Tayib," she'd say, and I'd rush past her and swoop down the stairs.

Danny and his mother rented our first floor in the summer of 1980. She was a bartender, sleeping until noon in a room adjacent to Danny's. When Danny and I triumphantly freed Lady from Donkey Kong, she'd yell at us in a scratchy voice to keep it down. Sometimes, there'd be a man with her, and he'd loom in the doorframe in his plaid boxers and bare chest, telling us to knock it off.

We were ten years old and Danny was crazy about *He-Man* action figures. He'd pull me by the sleeve into his room and make me play Skeletor before letting me at his video games. The funny thing was Danny's He-Man never tried to vanquish my Skeletor, despite my best efforts to lay ruin to his forts. Danny enjoyed forming treaties like those we'd learned in Social Studies. He'd say in a solemnly grown-up voice, "Accept these terms, sir, or face dire consequences."

I'd choose the latter, but he'd say in his whiny real-voice, "No, Sameer! You're supposed to agree to the terms."

He wore clunky-framed glasses and couldn't hit a baseball to save his life. When he got excited, his oversized White Sox cap shifted all the way around until the bill faced backwards. He was the only kid the neighborhood bullies enjoyed tormenting more than me.

When they were short on players, they'd call us over. "Hey, Ay-rab!" And to Danny, they'd yell, "You, too, faggot! You wanna play?"

They'd position us in the outfield to retrieve fly balls from a neighbor's yard, or ones that skipped off the hoods of parked cars. I didn't mind jogging past bungalows with gleaming lawns and narrow driveways. I didn't care much about playing, but Danny could barely contain his excitement. He'd try to high-five the boys, and they'd just wave him away like they were swatting flies.

Back then, I couldn't figure out Danny's obsession with baseball when his room was filled to the hilt with every action toy and video game manufactured back then. My mother figured she could buy a few pairs of jeans or a nice sweater for me to wear on eid instead of squandering money on one monster truck. At Christmas we didn't have a tree with mounting presents, but my father convinced my mother that purchasing one toy for their eight-year-old son from Toys R Us would not incur Allah's wrath. When we got there, she clucked her tongue and stared at parents pushing carts brimming with stuffed animals, board games, and snow sleds down every aisle.

"Ya haram! What a waste of money! Kids are starving in the mokhayamat," she'd lament. "Do you know how many refugee kids don't have a decent pair of shoes?"

Against one wall in Danny's room was a mid-sized shelf with the entire *Hardy Boys* series and an illustrated *Treasure Island*, which I'd pull out and read in a corner of his room when he was acting like a baby. If I threatened to leave, he'd beg me to stay. I'd settle back down on the floor while he looked at me with wary eyes behind those goofy glasses, afraid I'd still make good on my threat.

In the winter, I'd run down to Danny's in thick tube socks and my father's house slippers on frigid Saturday mornings. Danny wore green and brown turtlenecks that made him look like a giant bobble head.

That Christmas, Danny's uncle Paul moved in. His mother knocked on our back door to let my parents know her kid brother would be staying with them for a while. She brought a tin of red and green sprinkled shortbread cookies.

"It's only for a few months," she told my parents. "Just until he gets back on his feet."

"Family very good," my mother said with a wide smile, straddling baby Leena on her hip. Then, in Arabic to my father, "Ahsan min zalama. Better than strange men in her bed." She continued to smile innocently at Danny's mother.

My father said nothing. We both looked away when Danny's mother caught us staring at her large breasts straining against her red cashmere sweater. She had a pin in the shape of a giant gift bow secured to the fabric where her bosom began to swell.

Danny's uncle Paul was tall and lanky, with a small paunch that protruded when he leaned back and locked his fingers around the back of his head. In our enclosed back porch, he'd smoke Camels and talk with my father about the "crisis in the Middle East." My father stood there cradling two bags of groceries he'd brought home from his store. Paul scratched the bridge of his nose with a tobacco-stained finger when he spoke about Vietnam where he'd served for two years. He was a member of the last combat troops to be withdrawn in '73.

I eavesdropped as my father repeated some of Paul's stories to my mother. Though I vaguely understood as I listened through their bedroom door, I knew my father was leaving a lot of stuff out.

"Allahu samihna," my mother would say. "God forgive us all."

I could not see their faces, but I imagined my mother's eyes were wet. She had spent her childhood in a Palestinian refugee camp in Lebanon where she carried her good shoes to school to avoid raw sewage from splattering them. She and dozens of children crammed under a tent in a makeshift school for a few hours of lessons every day. Once a month, members of the United Nations Relief and Works Agency used the space for distributing sacks of wheat, rice, and sugar and checking children for tuberculosis.

"If I hadn't met your father, I would have rotted there," she told me, straightening my collar before I headed to school. Then she'd hold me a little longer, gripping my shoulders and gazing into my eyes until I looked down at my brown leather shoes..

* * *

Danny was thrilled to have his uncle around and wasn't so keen on inviting me over anymore. One morning, I knocked anyway, and he poked his head out the door like a rooster. "What?"

"Is that Suh-Meer?" his uncle called from inside. "Let him in, Danny-Boy."

He opened the door just wide enough for me to slip through, my elbow scraping the lock plate. "You can't stay long. Uncle Paul and me are planning stuff," he said.

On New Year's Eve, Danny and his uncle were at our back door. My mother stood facing them, her lips pursed in disapproval as Paul tried to hand my father a six-pack of Budweiser to ring in 1981.

"Thank you. We don't drink alcohol," my father politely said.

Danny pulled me aside to boast. "Uncle Paul's taking me to the Museum of Science and Industry to see the trains."

I watched my parents standing awkwardly, then I looked at Paul, his face flushed with many beers, his eyes glistening with merriment, and I wished I had different parents.

* * *

I didn't see Danny much after that and only in school. When Spring Training commenced, even the bullies wondered about Danny.

"Where's your faggot-friend, camel jockey?" they'd shout as I whizzed by them on my bike, nearly careening into a parked car when one of them charged me.

Danny's mother started waitressing to pay for secretarial school. She still tended bar on weekends. His uncle couldn't hold down a job and watched Danny during his mother's double shifts. Through the bathroom vent, I could hear muffled arguing between Danny's mother and uncle and the back door slamming. Sometimes, I thought I heard crying, but it didn't sound like it was coming from a woman.

At school, Danny would lay his head on his desk until the teacher tapped his shoulder. He sometimes missed a few days, and when I'd ask him about it, he said it was because of bronchitis. I figured it was something white people got—like asthma.

Paul still smoked on the porch and outside when all you needed was a light jacket. He was usually barefoot and his Levis jeans were frayed and hung low on his gaunt waist. He looked at me with hollow eyes, like he'd been in a dark room. He seemed annoyed when I said hello as though he'd been pondering something important, and I'd disturbed him.

"What? Oh, hey there, Suh-meer." He'd stub out his cigarette in an overflowing tin ashtray and absent-mindedly kick an empty Budweiser can from a pile he'd left on the porch. I'd pick them up and smell their sweet-metallic tabs, before swiftly discarding them in the alley so my mother wouldn't see.

***

It was my turn to be smug when Danny knocked on my door one Saturday morning in April. "What do you want?"

"You wanna come over"? He was chewing the neckline of his Superman t-shirt. He looked thinner with dark circles under his eyes like scuff marks.

"Only for an hour, habibi," my mother said. "We're driving to Ashland for shoes".

In his room, I picked up Skeletor as usual, but Danny just sat on his bed with his baseball mitt, listlessly rubbing his thumb against the worn-down leather.

"Play whatever you want," he said dully.

"Neat!" I gave Skeletor a friendly toss across the room. I planted myself squarely in front of Danny's twenty-inch television and concentrated hard on his Atari. After a while, his uncle opened the door.

"Hey there, Suh-meer." He tousled my hair and sat next to Danny. "Hey, Danny-Boy."

"You can't come in here when I have friends over," Danny said. "Mom said so."

I paused. I had been silently pressing buttons with eyes glued to the screen. Danny's tense voice shook like a plate rattling in a sink.

"You know something, Suh-meer? Time to go home, buddy," his uncle said. "Danny's not feelin' too good."

I sprung up from the floor, but Danny leapt off his bed and grabbed my wrist. I couldn't help thinking of the neighborhood bullies calling us "a couple of homos" when they saw us sitting side by side on my front stairs. I shook free.

"No, I'm not sick," Danny pleaded. "Really, Sameer, you can stay."

I was a little scared. "I think my mom's calling me. We're going to Ashland to buy shoes," I said, and though it was completely true, it sounded flimsy and weak.

Danny and his uncle were cemented to that space on the floor of his bedroom. He gave his uncle a stiff sidelong glance then looked straight at me.

For a long time after, Danny's look clung to me like photographs on the yellowed, sticky pages of an old-fashioned album. It was a look of fear and shame so thick it made Danny's eyelids droop behind his glasses; the look of someone who'd been through a war—the same look his uncle Paul had, revealing he'd endured as much pain as he'd inflicted.

That summer of 1981, Danny and his mother moved out of our first floor apartment after his uncle Paul shot himself on a toilet at a Shell gas station.

In September of 1982, I was outside carving my name under the front stairs when my mother's shrieks brought me running into our house. She was standing in front of our television set as news broke of the massacre of men, women and children in the Sabra and Shatila refugee camps in west Beirut. On the floor, my baby sister was also shrieking and pumping her fists, terrified and confused by our mother who was clawing at her floral housedress until she tore it down the middle. I swiftly carried Leena away and soothed her in her crib until she fell asleep.

When I returned to the front room, I was afraid to touch my mother who had crumbled to the floor. Her eyes had become dull and empty as she stared at the images on the screen. I sat beside her and we stayed like that long after the sun set. The only light emanated from the T.V. and the only sounds drifting inside the room came from my mother's whimpers and the voice of the American reporter standing amidst the carnage. We did not speak until my father came home. He lifted my mother and carried her like a limp doll to their bedroom. She couldn't speak for two days afterwards.

Twenty years later, I remember that day when I visit my parents. I climb up their back porch, two steps at a time. The stairs are worn down after another decade of paint has chipped away.

I remember Danny, too, and his *He-Man* action figures and treaties for peace.

Before I reach the landing, I hear my aged mother on her new cellphone, chattering with a relative overseas. I turn the doorknob to enter the kitchen. For a moment, Danny's face appears then quickly slides away like a fly ball we used to chase before losing it to the gutter.

American Dollars

On the last day of Ramadan, we stood in the square, unsure what to do with our hands as we abstained from smoking and drinking coffee until sunset, and silently watched Abu Yusuf. In his customary act of charity, he peeled off paper bills from a thick wad and hold them out for us. Not shekels, but American dollars printed on dull green paper with an intricate design and an older, distinguished-looking man with a trimmed beard positioned stolidly off-center.

Abu Yusuf's heavy girth forced his legs apart as he stood, feet firmly planted on the gravel. He was a tall man with strong, square shoulders, amply filling out a suit jacket without sagging. He held out his hand and we moved forward to claim his zakat that we knew was nowhere near the properly extracted percentage of his wealth from his supermarket chain in America. We, who could aspire to be no more than village merchants and peddlers, fantasized about those prosperous stores in a lavish city as our wives placed leftover bowls of addas soup in front of us on the floor-height table. Still, we—thirty, forty and fifty-year old men, half of us already grandfathers—stepped forward like small children and accepted his charity. He squinted at our faces and smiled and we took some consolation in his losing his eyesight.

When he was finished, Abu Yusuf climbed into his Cadillac, a brand new plum-red 1983 DeVille he had shipped from overseas. Some of us had driven in it with our loads of vegetables or sacks of wheat from the hisbah and we climbed into the back seat and navigated Abu Yusuf to our small beit.

Though he held no official position—he was not the mukhtar of the village, nor was he chairman of any municipality—Abu Yusuf was probably the most important man we admitted to knowing. And he was very much so that we took perverse pleasure in envying and loathing him as a fellow countryman who'd made his fortune in America while we labored like mules and were prisoners of the Occupation which had closed us inside a sliver of rocky territory far from the Mediterranean Sea which the yahood could see from their coastal houses that lined Haifa and Acre—our stolen cities.

The day after he distributed his dollars to us was Eid al-Fitr and Abu Yusuf slaughtered a kharoof and hung the sheep's body to bleed on a loquat tree in his front yard. He distributed the meat to a family in Al Uma'ari camp, a widow with five children.

On his way home, Abu Yusuf struck and killed Taha, Abu Ribhi's son, his youngest. The baker, who had been smoking outside his store, witnessed it and helped Abu Yusuf carefully lift the boy and place him gently in the backseat. The baker climbed into the front passenger seat and Abu Yusuf drove to Hadassah Hospital where the doctors only spoke Hebrew and they had to find a nurse or an orderly who could speak a mixture of English and Arabic to explain how dire the boy's condition was. According to the baker, the boy had not been breathing when they lay him across the leather seat. There was no blood except for a trickle down one of the boy's ears and scratches on the side of his face.

"Kul jismo muksoor," the baker told us. "His body's all broken. Allah have mercy on his soul."

We shook our heads and the next morning walked silently to Abu Ribhi's beit to mourn with him for three days. Um Ribhi, his wife, had beaten her own face when Abu Yusuf and the baker had returned to their house without their son. It was midnight when Abu Yusuf returned to the village, only to drive the parents back to Hadassah for them to properly identify the body before the yahoodi doctors would release it.

By the third day of azza, our conversations grew louder and less strained until Abu Yusuf showed up to pay his respects. We collectively parted the way for him to take a seat among us. We returned to silence and sipped bitter, unsweetened coffee, and tried hard to ignore the low moaning of Um Ribhi and her relatives who had travelled from another village to be with her.

Abu Ribhi's middle sons refilled our tiny cups, the dark-brown liquid pouring out like a contaminated stream of sewage running through a refugee camp. His oldest son Ribhi, sitting beside his father, glared at Abu Yusuf across the semicircle of men on roped stools. Abu Ribhi gently patted his son's knee to placate him. Ribhi's slender body leaned forward and we sat tensely as though he might pounce like a tiger. Ribhi had recently passed his towjeehi exams with more than passing grades and would begin his science track for the next two years before attending university. When he finally leaped up, he spat dramatically on the ground and kicked a few empty stools before disappearing into Abu Ribhi's beit. We hid our smug approval with more sips of coffee and drags on our cigarettes.

"I didn't see the boy," Abu Yusuf announced. "He appeared out of nowhere."

We believed he had not seen Taha because he refused to permanently wear the glasses he brought from the States in 1982—a wire pair of half-moon lenses with a bridge. He kept them folded in his front suit pocket. Today he was wearing them and he continually touched them as though reassuring himself of their existence and that they had not disappeared from his tanned face.

"It's in Allah's hands." This was from Abu Mazen, who sold smoked and blanched watermelon seeds and mixed roasted nuts. "It was his time. Inshallah his soul find an easy flight to our Lord."

The rest of us nodded and tapped the rims of our tiny cups.

"I turned the corner and he jumped in front of me," Abu Yusuf continued as though he were giving a testimony. He was not looking at anyone in particular and we seemed to have disappeared and were invisible as we always were when Abu Yusuf was present. He stood up and faced Abu Ribhi, pulling him up by his shoulders and hastily brushed his cheek against each of the bereaved father's and marched away. We listened for the roar of the engine and the crunching of tires as Abu Yusuf pulled away.

Soon after, Um Ribhi stumbled out of her beit and lurched forward, her arms cut and bleeding. Her sisters chased her, wailing, and tried to pry the paring knife from Um Ribhi's fingers. Abu Ribhi buried his face in his hands and sobbed.

* * *

When the forty days of mourning were over, we approached Abu Ribhi. "You should not delay this matter any longer," we told Abu Ribhi. He seemed to have dwarfed to half his height and his shoulders were stooped.

"What's right is right," we vehemently declared. Our indignation was easy because we had not remained awake with Abu Ribhi on the night before the burial, observing and lightly touching the young bruised skin of his son, his fingers hovering over the spots where splintered bones pierced through. Abu Nidal was the only other man among us who had lost a son. Amer's body had not collided with steel and tire, but had been ripped open by a machine gun during a raid by the yahoodi soldiers. A photograph of Amer hung in an enormous gilded frame in Abu Nidal's sitting room. There was no retribution for his family, or any family of martyrs. Yet, Abu Ribhi had every right to recourse for his son, struck down by one man's vanity.

"You must request a'twa," we insisted. "A sit-down is necessary to demand your compensation. Justice—it's your right."

"Inshallah, inshallah," Abu Ribhi said.

"I can arrange a'twa," Abu Mazen offered. "On Friday, after the evening prayers, come to my home and we'll settle this matter. I'll speak with Abu Yusuf, inshallah."

Several of us offered ourselves as witnesses for the event. We insolently and quite dangerously believed that Abu Yusuf had wronged us, too. It was a bittersweet indulgence like the pit of a plum sucked clean of its succulent juices.

"Inshallah, inshallah," Abu Ribhi said again, glancing over our shoulders at the open window of the barranda where his wife had been watching our small congregation.

* * *

Each party involved in the dispute would have a representative to help mediate and mend as much as was humanly possible in the loss of a child by utter negligence. Abu Mazen's eldest brother would mediate. Abu Ribhi, still jittery and unable to make swift decisions, deferred to the rest of us to find an honorable man to speak on his behalf. It took no time at all to settle on Abu Wisam, a local carpenter. It was easy to trust a man who worked with his hands.

On his terrace that faced a small vineyard, Abu Mazen served tea with mint leaves floating on the surface. Ripened green grapes hung heavily from their vines and the bougainvillea grew madly over stones walls that bordered Abu Mazen's two dunum of land. We waited for our drinks to cool before nursing the small glasses without handles. We chain-smoked, lighting one cigarette with the butt of the previous one, our eyes flickering up from our feet when a car approached.

Almost an hour later, we heard the slam of a car door and Abu Yusuf appeared. He was, expectedly, not alone. Sheikh Issa shuffled alongside him, the hem of his gellabiya dragging along the ground. The old man waved at us from a distance as though hailing someone to stop in their tracks. We all stood, though our spirits instantly deflated by this new prospect. Abu Yusuf had chosen our highly revered minister to represent him. Even the carpenter was no match for such grand piety. It was a clever move, we conceded. The mosque was in disrepair. The tiles in the common sink had come undone and were chipped from erosion, and we knew how eager the sheikh was to replace the existing windows with stained glass.

Abu Yusuf shook hands with the host Abu Mazen and the carpenter, and gave the rest of us stiff nods. He approached Abu Ribhi with arms wide, swallowing the gaunt man in his embrace. Abu Ribhi looked guilty and pathetic as though he were the one who had come for penitence. Abu Yusuf touched his eye glasses as he sat on a stool, finally level with the rest of us.

A second round of tea was served and we waited for the carpenter to open dialogue. But it was Sheikh Issa who interjected—a benign usurper—and officiated the proceedings.

"May Allah grant us all the wisdom and humility to see our wrongs and rectify them so we find everlasting life in his kingdom," the sheikh began.

We sat stone-still while the men negotiated. Sheikh Keefah finally determined the value of the young boy's life: five-thousand American dollars would be paid to Abu Ribhi. Abu Yusuf stood up and pulled a thick white envelope with a wide rubber band from inside his jacket pocket and removed a wad of bills in the same manner he did every eid when we huddled around him for our shares. He moistened his thumb and counted.

When the correct amount had been doled out, we noticed nearly half of the original wad remained and Abu Yusuf quickly slid the money back into the envelope and fastened the rubber band around it. He inserted the folded bills into the bereaved man's shirt pocket before kissing him on both cheeks. One of the young men helped the sheikh to his feet and we watched him and Abu Yusuf climb into the DeVille and drive away.

In our own homes, we contemplated all that Abu Ribhi could buy and pay off with his newly acquired sum of money. Our wives just sucked their teeth and declared that the best use of that money would be to line a chicken coop or wipe his children's asses with it.

We only nodded, silently calculating.

Life Springs from the Dead Sea

"And what is your business here in Israel?" the man behind the plated glass window asks me.

"I'm visiting relatives," I say. The muscles in my neck feel like thick braided ropes, tight with twelve hours of jetlag. I work hard to keep from wincing in pain while the middle-aged man with piercing blue eyes and a closely shaven head interrogates me.

"This is your first visit to Israel?"

"Yes," I answer for the third time.

He looks down at my passport as though my image might somehow morph if my answer changes. He holds it in one hand and writes notes on a form with the other. I can see a tiny hairless spot on his forearm that could be scar tissue.

I don't give him a polite smile but I don't defiantly stare either. I look around customs at Ben Gurion International Airport. Beyond the row of plated-glass cubicles where attendants open and stamp passports, a visitor's oasis—once you can pass through—stands brightly on the other side of customs, an Israeli flag vertically dropped from the expansive ceiling. The airport is clean and efficient except for the section in customs devoted exclusively to passengers who are discernibly Arab. They are herded to one side while others swiftly move through the security queues: men in yarmulkes and their women in long skirts; Filipinos with tiny crucifix necklaces; fashionably dressed Europeans; and white nuns.

I'm tempted to ask the man behind the window about this disparity.

Don't antagonize them or they'll put you on the next plane out of there, my aunt Fahima told me during a farewell dinner. *They look for any excuse to keep falasteeniya from entering the country.*

So I remain quiet, speaking only when spoken to. A woman in a floral hijab with three children stands behind me, cradling the youngest of them in her arms. The toddler's mouth is half-open and her eyelids flutter in half-dreams. She startles, eyes creak open then droop again in slumber. The woman's face is tense and tired, but she gives me a reassuring smile.

"Be patient," she whispers. "You'll get through."

To the customs officer, I repeat, "My grandfather's name is—was—Othman Izzadine. He died in Hebron."

"Why have you travelled here now?" He glances at my passport again. "You will be thirty-three in a month."

"It was my mother's wish."

"To visit Israel?"

"To visit her family," I say evenly. "Her hometown." I twirl my wedding band.

"Is she traveling with you?"

"She's dead." Something balloons in my chest and I breathe deeply. I've announced this only a few times to strangers since her funeral and sharing this information with an Israeli security officer seems unsanctified.

"So you wait until after she died to visit?" There's a dangerous twinkle in his eyes.

I stay quiet. I stink of sweat and a faint perfume I applied ten hours ago.

He smiles and tells me to wait a moment. He disappears through a door behind him that has a sign in Hebrew.

All the signs are menacing here. In Chicago, I'd seen plenty of Hebrew signs with the same squared letters on hospitals and temples. But, here in this airport, they are all commands and warnings. They direct me where to go, where to stand. All of them contain English and some contain Arabic translations, but there's a palpable severity—something formidable hanging over the airport.

The man returns with my passport but does not give it back to me.

"Please wait in Line 3. Over there."

After twenty more minutes, a man in a navy-blue uniform instructs me to follow him to an area with a desk and chairs. Another round of interrogation begins. It's been two hours since my plane has landed. I worry about Hamza, the hired driver, waiting for me, wondering why I haven't emerged from the terminal.

"What is your business in Israel?" His face is pleasantly calm and he smiles after each of my responses. I can smell his pine after-shave, can see where he's nicked the skin directly below his ear with a blade. It's a tiny crust of blood—imperceptible if not for how close we are sitting across from each other.

"I'm visiting relatives."

"How long are you staying?"

"Two weeks."

"That's not very long." He licks his fingertip and turns the pages of my passport.

I'm not sure whether to comment since it's not a direct question. The officer looks up at me expectantly. His eyes are as dark as mine, his brows thick, yet groomed.

"I have a job in Chicago," I tell him. I look for the hijabi woman with three children. She has advanced to the glass-plated window. She's put the toddler down so that she can provide passports and answer questions. The toddler vehemently tugs her hand, inconsolable after being awakened and now subjected to standing in a line with her siblings.

"Your job is able to dispense with you for two weeks?" The officer pauses to examine a stamp from Heathrow after my college graduation. "What do you do?"

"Hospital administration."

"With whom are you staying during your short visit?"

"My mother's brother." I straighten up in my chair and roll away the fatigue in my shoulders.

"Name and address?"

"Rizq Abu Rasheed." I can't remember the street. Without asking for permission, I search through my purse until my fingers graze a tightly folded sheet of paper. It takes a second to unfold and I show the officer. "El Sharafa Street, El Bireh." I cannot comprehend how houses in Palestine do not have numbers.

Everybody knows everybody, my cousin Taha told me on our way to O'Hare International Airport. That was twelve hours ago, but seems like days now.

So what if there's an emergency? A fire or something? I had insisted, turning the volume down on a lewd rap song playing on his car radio. I wanted to admit to him how anxious I was to be traveling there alone, a place all of our parents called *el bilad*—the old country—and that's what their children called it, too, even if some of us had never seen it.

They're stone houses, Taha said. *The only thing that will destroy them is an American bulldozer, habibti.* He snorted in disgust.

Okay. What if someone needs to go to a hospital? I asked.

They call an ambulance and tell them 'it's the beit next to Dakhilallah's villa—the one with the almond grove.' The paramedic says, 'Ah, Dakhilallah's? His almonds are the best in the balad. We'll be right there!' Taha laughed at his own joke.

I was not amused as I rested my head against the cool window. *That's grim*, I told Taha. A billboard for cellphones loomed over the I-90 exit to O'Hare.

The temperature of the airport is very cool and goose pimples rise on my skin as the Israeli officer says to me, "I thought you were visiting Hebron.

"No. The other man asked for my maternal grandfather's name," I slowly tell him, dangerously close to becoming uncooperative. "He lived in Hebron. I'm visiting other relatives in El Bireh."

I remember my aunt's warning about ways they might try to trip me up though I have nothing to hide. I have no connections to this place, no attachment except what belongs to my mother.

They try to treek you, Aunt Fahima had cautioned in English. *Be con-sees-tant.*

The security officer hands me my passport. "Enjoy your visit to Israel," he says and disappears behind a door.

* * *

Hamza, the driver, has been waiting for me outside a pair of automatic sliding doors. He stubs out his cigarette on the pavement and extends his hand and vigorously shakes mine. A queue of taxicabs stretches behind Hamza's car.

"I am Hamza," he says. "Madeeha, is it? Welcome home, sister."

"I was worried you'd left," I tell him. "I was in there for two hours."

"That's nothing," Hamza informs me. "Some people wait four to eight hours to get through. I've done this for many years. I know how long it takes so I don't have to sit around for too long." His face glistens with sweat as he gathers my luggage and stores them in the trunk of his cab. He juts his chin at the other cabs. "One of those poor bastards has been waiting since morning."

Outside the night is strangely still, like I've stepped into a new world. The clamor of the airport—customs, security officers, crying babies—is sucked back behind me. All at once, I am relieved, yet still shackled to some ominous entity that knows I don't belong here and will be closely watching me.

"The last time I saw your mother—may Allah have mercy on her soul—was ten years ago," Hamza tells me, holding the passenger door open for me.

Ten years. In ten years, I earned two degrees, travelled to England, got married. Ten years ago, I had just finished my Bachelor's and my mother had begged me to accompany her to Palestine as a graduation gift. I chose London and Bath because my father wouldn't be in either of those places.

"How did those iklab treat you in there?" he asks me. "Those dogs can wear you down with their questions."

"They kept asking the same ones—just restated differently each time."

"That's their way," Hamza explains. "They figure if they hassle falasteeniya like you who have U.S. passports you'll stop trying to visit. It's a clever method of reducing interest and residence here." He pulls a pack of cigarettes tucked in his shirt pocket. He coaxes one out and lights it with the cab lighter. "I couldn't stand it anymore, you know, and left for five years. I moved to Brazil and lived with my sister and her husband. He's a big shot university professor in Sao Paulo." He took a drag on his cigarette. "I had no idea how large the Palestinian community is there. Sometimes it felt like I never left this place. Same squalor, same corruption—different language."

I roll down my window. The night smells of the sun, like it's been baked into it. A blanket of stars blinks closer than the aloof ones I'm used to in the States. "How far are we from my uncle's home?" I ask Hamza.

"At this time of night, about thirty minutes."

Hamza drives me through Qalandiya checkpoint. In the dark, the political graffiti is eerie, large banners of Arabic words sprawled across the dividing wall. I see the oversized-painted faces of children with enormous tears and small fingers making the peace sign.

"So you're married?" Hamza asks me. "Why didn't your husband accompany you?"

"He's traveling, too, for his work," I say. "He's a salesman. He's in California for a—what do you call it—a *mu'tamar*. A convention."

Seventy-two hours ago, it was hard to mask my discontent when Ata held me close, apologizing profusely for not being able to make this trip with me. His dry-cleaned shirts still in their thin plastic shields were draped over our bed. I leaned against the vanity dresser and watched him neatly roll his socks and underwear in a carry-on bag.

It's my turn, habibti, he told me. *The senior guys have already gone so they send the rookie.*

He gathered me up and squeezed my ass. *I will miss this and the rest of you.* Then he held me at arm's length and looked into my face. *Wallahi, your mother would be proud of you, Madeeha. Doing this for her—it's important. I can't believe you're only staying for two weeks.*

I gave him a sullen stare. My mother was both surprised and relieved that I had chosen to marry someone arrabi. She'd figured my father's behavior—his leaving her without a proper divorce and marrying again to someone half his age—had tainted my view of all Arab men. And it had for a while until the end of my freshman year at DePaul when I'd secretly dated a white guy for months before he dumped me for his high school sweetheart who'd returned home after flunking out of an east-coast university. It was painfully clear that most men were emotionally unavailable and capable of hurting me no matter what their heritage.

But then I met Ata, a business major at NIU whose eyebrows rose up when he laughed or became concerned. It seemed incongruous with a man's face and I knew I could trust him. My mother had been pleased he was educated, and was not another liquor store heir in the most dangerous neighborhoods of Chicago. Ata was unlike some of the young Arab men who'd been bequeathed—regardless of their consent—with a business in which a gun lay concealed beneath the cash register.

I realize how hard it will be dealing with your father, Ata told me that night, zipping up his bag and dropping it outside of our bedroom door. He pulled me close again. *He's still your father, you know. Besides, you'll see some terrific things over there.*

I'm not sure how much sightseeing I'll get in. I'd really like to see the Dead Sea, I said.

Now there's a positive attitude! Ata teased. *I wish we could see it together.*

There had been a special on *National Geographic* that my mother and I had been watching one evening after she showed me how to properly steam the cabbage for malfoof—Ata's favorite meal. It was shortly after we were married. Scientists had discovered craters brimming with freshwater and bacteria at the bottom of the Dead Sea. The possibility of life was no longer a theory.

I touched my husband's cheek and rubbed his chin full of tiny black stubble, and kissed him hard on the mouth. *I'll miss you.*

Yes you will, he told me and finished packing.

* * *

Hamza slows down and makes a U-turn on a street lined with small houses and storefronts. He pulls up to a six-flat building and shadowy trees in the front yard. A few of the windows are lit like pairs of winking eyes. The night has cooled down and crickets chirp in crevices I can't see.

"Wislat! Wislat!" A woman's voice cries out. "She's arrived! She's arrived!"

I hear the slapping of sandals and clacking of heels before I see bodies. I roll my suitcase over the uneven pavement that leads to the main entrance of the building. My relatives descend upon me like bats. In the darkness, I glimpse teary eyes in hijab-bordered faces, hands reaching out to take my luggage, white teeth smiling. I'm swept up and herded into a staircase to the second floor.

My uncle's flat is small, but cheerful. Framed photographs of wedding parties and black-and-white portraits of single men and women barely leave any inch of space on one wall. In the upper row, I see a picture of my mother holding me up to the camera. I'm not yet a year old and my chubby arms are spread wide, my small fists clenched in a combination of delight and fear as my mother pumps me up and down. I have the same picture framed and sitting on my wooden dresser in my bedroom back home.

Straight ahead and hanging above a doorframe to what appears to be a small bedroom is a gold-gilded verse from the Qur'an. There are several of these mounted verses lining a narrow hallway.

"Ghalabooki al yahood?" Khalo Rizq asks me. "Did those Jews give you trouble?" He guides me by the elbow onto the enclosed barranda. From the window, I catch the taillights of Hamza's car speeding away.

"Sit, sit," he instructs me. "How have you been, *khalo*?" He has my mother's wide eyes and the crinkle between the eyebrows. His lips are thinner, but they are quick to smile like my mother's.

"Fine," I say. "Busy with work." I feel awkward, out of place. I am his adult niece and have never had a conversation with him in my life.

"Wallahi, your mother's passing," he tells me. "It has been very hard on us. I wish I could have been there to bury her."

"At least she went quickly," a woman interrupts. She is my uncle's wife's sister Suad, whom I have only just met. She sits on a chair beside me and leans over to clutch my armrest. She speaks as though she was present at my mother's passing.

Khalo Rizq nods his head like he's trying to convince himself.

"Some people suffer for a long time after it happens," Suad adds.

My uncle looks at me for affirmation that is was quick.

"Yes," I say. "Elhamdulillah."

My mother's stroke was swift like a power surge flicking all the lights off then on again. Except she never regained consciousness and died within hours of arriving at Silver Cross hospital. My father called, but I refused to speak with anyone overseas. Ata and my aunt Howaida fielded all communications until I was ready.

You need to come home, were my father's first words on the line when Ata handed me his cellphone.

I wondered whose home he meant. Two weeks had passed since I buried my mother. Ten years since I saw my father.

News of my father's second wife had been a shock to me. It had only been two years since his sudden departure when he had hauled a single suitcase out of the bedroom he had stopped sleeping in with my mother and rolled it through the garage. He had barely looked at me that day, mumbling he'd had enough and couldn't live like this anymore. I was sixteen, thin and tall, excelling in all of my classes and working part-time at Wendy's. I had finally gotten my license and inherited my mother's tidy old Camry. I didn't know at the time that his abandonment wasn't the worst of it, that this new betrayal would be the thing that irrevocably wounded my mother and me: he had taken on another wife while still married to my mother.

This latest scandal had not been delivered privately nor discreetly, but in the presence of a half-dozen arabiyat crowded in my mother's townhouse for their monthly version of girls' night. We received the news together which was far worse as my mother had always been a buffer between me and hard times. When I was a child, she kept me home on days when Christmas parties were planned at school and the other mothers came in to help the teacher coordinate crafts and pass out cheap gifts like bingo sets and fruit-smelling erasers. In second grade, I came crying into the kitchen one day after discovering I had been the only girl in our homeroom class who wasn't invited to Caley's birthday at the roller rink. My mother kept me home the day after the party so I wouldn't have to hear my fair-skinned, freckle-faced classmates boasting and reinventing all the fun they had. As much as she could, my mother managed to wedge herself between me and heartache. But she couldn't shield me from the greatest one and I stood alongside the other gawking women as a witness to her shame.

Her best friend Kareema mock-bit a finger in alarm while the other women gathered around my mother. Their gracious and sometimes impish smiles tightened into feral, teeth-baring glowers. A sister of theirs had been attacked, injured, and now they huddled close around my mother's chair, ears prickling and alert.

I was eighteen years old, two months away from graduation, and didn't understand what had transpired during the seconds it took me to deliver a steel pan of steaming kufta to the dining room table, set up like a buffet for this gathering. I paused mid-step and turned, careful of the tomato juice still simmering and sloshing in the pan. Aunt Howaida pushed past me from the hallway bathroom and the juice streamed down the side of the pan and seeped between my fingers.

Mustaheel! Impossible! she called out before reaching the women. Unlike me, she had obviously figured out the catastrophe that cast a shadow over my mother's dinner party like a patch of cumulus clouds obstructing the sun when the sky had been clear for hours.

Impossible, Aunt Howaida declares again. *How can he have taken a second wife?*

What did you expect? a woman whose name I always forget said. This was the nature of these arabiyat—these women were sympathetic and enraged at the sleight one of them had endured, and in the same breath they chastised and implicated her in her own demise. *They've been apart for—what—six years now?*

The women began debating this and referred to my mother in the third person as though she were a victim in an article they were skimming in a newspaper, commenting quickly without absorbing actual details.

I found this unsettling and hurriedly set the pan down, no longer concerned about splattering my mother's linen tablecloth or myself. I pushed through the women in the semicircle, but I didn't know what I had meant to do. I flopped down on the floor in front of my mother's chair and took her hands—helplessly folded in her lap—and held them.

* * *

The last time we had spoken was a month before she died. My father had called to speak with Ata, who maintained a steady communication with his absentee father-in-law. It's Ata's nature to keep the peace, to be exhaustively diplomatic when an impasse in the war between my father and me could not be surmounted. At the end of their conversation, if I was home, Ata would hand me his cell phone, his eyes beseeching me to be kind.

For your mother, my father was saying through Ata's cellphone, thousands of miles and oceans away, his voice without treble. *Her family needs to see you here. To ease their grief.*

Ten weeks later, I am sitting on a worn-down chair across from my mother's youngest brother while his wife's sister asks me about clan members in the States. His wife Nadira heats up a plate of yellow squash mahshi in their tiny kitchen. There is another chair and a thin floor mattress with a folded red-velvet prayer rug on its edge. The only light comes from the half-moon that sits low in the night sky—lower than I'd ever seen back home in Chicago—and a small lamp Khalo Rizq flicks on. The top panel of windows that enclose this space can be opened up. There are no mesh screens so mosquitoes enter and hover lazily near the dim lamp. The sweet scent of heliotrope drifts in, and I detect stalks of spearmint.

Nadira brings me a plate of mahshi and I eat one stuffed squash and take two bites of a second one. She is followed by two teenage girls whose heads are now bare indoors. One of them places a small wooden table before me and the other sets pocket-bread on it. They are all smiles and nods as they settle on the floor mattress, their legs tucked beneath them, hidden by their long dishdashas.

"Wallahi, I'm tired," I apologize when my uncle wife's observes the remaining three squash on my plate. Their cooked skin is still bright, but no longer glossy in the tomato sauce.

"*Yeee!* You barely ate, ya binit!" Nadira admonishes. She has an oval face like a perfect pearl and just as fair.

"Leave her be, ya marra!" My uncle scolds his wife. "She'll have her appetite back once she's rested."

"Sallim idayki," I say to Nadira. I can see how much she enjoys serving others and hovers until every need is met. "Thank you. It was delicious." I stand up to signal I'm ready to be escorted to my room. I'm glad it's night so I can more easily adjust to the eight-hour time difference.

"Before you go, *khalo*," my uncle says, gesturing for me to sit down again. "Let's have a prayer for your mother."

I'm startled at first. It has been more than four months. Khalo Rizq's eyes are pleading. I realize that I have buried my mother, that I have seen her naked body on a metal embalming table in the Hann Funeral Home, where all deceased falasteeniya were tended. She was washed by my aunt Howaida and her friend Kareema who sat next to me at the wake, telling me over and over that she had always believed she would be the first to go, before my mother.

I sit down again.

Khalo Rizq didn't see the coffin, didn't hear the imam's instructions that we not cling to our grief because that merely torments the soul of the deceased instead of releasing it to find peace. My uncle didn't see where she was lowered into the musky earth of Evergreen Cemetery, in a section unofficially designated for Chicago Arabs. She is surrounded by those who died young and old from the same town, and near others from villages I wondered if she'd ever been to.

My uncle recites du'aa—supplications for the dead. My uncle's wife and her sister and daughters punctuate each one with *ameen*. I watch their bowed heads and folded hands across their stomachs and swallow a thick knot of grief.

Suad says good night and closes the door behind her. She lives a few houses down the street. Nadira locks the metal door after her sister leaves and shows me where I'll sleep.

I share it with my cousins Fadwa and Fatin, the teenagers who regard me, a hijab-less woman, with keen interest. We smile shyly at each other, me from the single bed one of them has given up to sleep on the opposite end of her sister's bed. Fadwa holds her sister's squirming feet still as she speaks to me.

"I bet you're already missing amarka, mish ah?" she asks. She has a disarming gap in her upper teeth and I worry I'll truthfully answer any question she asks because of it. Her black hair sweeps past her shoulders in waves tamed by the perpetual headscarf. "Nothing exciting happens here," she says miserably.

I consider all I know about the Occupation, suicide bombings, air raids, closed borders, and remain quiet and keep smiling.

"Do you work in amarka?" Fatin asks. She's lying on her stomach, propped up on her elbows. She's the younger sister. The same features have been dealt to her but with a lighter touch, and it's obvious she's the prettier one. The gap between her teeth is slighter and more sensuous.

"Yes. In a hospital."

"Are you a nurse?" Fadwa asks.

"No. I work in—" I fumble for the Arabic word for a*dministration*. "I'm responsible for keeping the hospital organized and running smoothly."

"Oh, like a *mudeera*"? Fatin suggests. "Like a manager?"

"Yes. A *mudeera*."

"Excellent! Azzeem!" They both declare, impressed.

"We wept for your mother," Fatin tells me. "We were much younger the last time she visited, but we remember how nice she was. Allah yarhamha."

"She brought us glittery pink backpacks," Fadwa adds.

"The kids at school envied us for a whole week," Fatin remembers. "Until Lama's uncle brought her a tacky coat with fur on its collar. Remember that, Fadwa?" She playfully wags her foot in her sister's face.

"Bas! Bas!" Fadwa scolds, clutching her foot. "Wallahi if you kick me in the middle of the night, you're gonna get it!"

"Good night," I say and lay on my back. A mosquito buzzes near my ear and I flick it away until my eyelids become heavy and I drift into a dreamless sleep.

The next morning brings a deluge of more relatives I've never met and some I've never heard of. Everyone is sad and polite and kisses both of my cheeks, holding me a few seconds longer, pressing me to them, wanting to ingest anything I might have brought of my mother with me. Their effusiveness, their intimate way of pulling me close as though needing to affirm they had perpetually lingered in some part of my mother's consciousness over the years and distance—that she hadn't forgotten them—did not surprise me. But, it did make me uncomfortable as I was an unworthy proxy for her love and esteem.

Some of the younger women who are my age wear fashionably wrapped headscarves while their mothers—first and second cousins to my mother—wear plain white hijab. I realize I'm the only woman with a bare head and I continuously tuck strands of my wavy hair behind my ears.

Nadira has laid out a delicious spread of fatayir: open-faced zaatar and olive oil bread, summac-spiced spinach pies, freshly fried falafel, hummus and lebanah. I'm hungry this morning and answer visitors' questions as best as I can between bites of food and sips of spearmint tea.

—How long was she in the hospital? Did she suffer?

—Did you hold three days of azza? She was a wonderful woman, after all.

—Is she in a Muslim cemetery? May Allah forgive al kafreen who lay beside her.

—Have you seen your father yet? His only daughter—may Allah keep you safe for each other!

The street outside the flat has become noisy with honking cars and laughing children. A vendor hails the ripeness of his tomatoes and I hear squeaky wheels as a cart is pushed. I want to escape the small parlor where visitors have crammed in to pay their respects. I want to lounge on the barranda, which faces east, gathering the full face of the sun at mid-morning.

Just before noon, I hear the muezzin's call to prayer and I'm filled with both a strange melancholy and solace. I've heard the same deep and resonant voice coming through my mother's stereo, from a cassette, as we broke our fast during Ramadan, and I heard the imam at the Bridgeview mosque recite the same salat call, but it has always been confined within the walls of the mosque—never resounding outside, washing over an entire town, echoing in the alleyways. I wish Ata were here.

* * *

By late afternoon, my father arrives with a diminutive woman, much younger than him. I suspect he has waited for most visitors to have come and gone so that we can speak in private.

He has aged as I had expected over a decade. He's heavier and looks whittled down—or maybe it's because he's gained weight. I rise up about an inch over him when I stand. His hair has thinned to a dull gray and he combs it over, but it doesn't hide the small brown spots on his scalp.

"How have you been, Madeeha?" he asks me in English. He tentatively opens his arms.

I step into his weak embrace and say, "I'm fine. Elhamdulillah."

The woman steps forward and grabs my arms. "Allah yarhamha your mother," she tells me, kissing me on both cheeks. "Mashallah, your daughter's quite pretty," she tells my father. She speaks in a heavy fellahi accent, crunching the consonant *k* into a *ch* sound. My mother would have mocked her speech.

"This is Basima," my father says, placing his hand on her shoulder. "I'm sure you heard all about her," he adds in English.

I refuse to be congenial. "Of course, I've heard all about Basima," I say in Arabic. Yet, my wickedness is lost upon this woman who continues to smile at me as though we are long lost relatives. Her white hijab swallows up most of her face; her large eyes glint like amber stones in two pools of water. I must admit she is a lovely woman.

"Why don't you take a stroll in the garden," Khalo Rizq suggests. "Come, please drink tea with my wife," he tells Basima who cheerfully nods and follows him to the kitchen where my uncle's wife is drying cups and saucers. She and her sister have been serving guests since this morning.

Like me, Nadira is unenthusiastic about this blithe and petite woman in her home, but doesn't refuse a guest. "How many spoons of sugar, sister?" I hear her ask before my father and I step out the back door.

In the yard, green velvet-skinned almonds hang from a tree. The fig tree is bare, its wide branches thick with dark leaves. A few wicker stools are underneath it and a small pile of roasted pumpkin seed husks is heaped near its trunk. A grapevine creeps over a stonewall between my uncle's building and the beit to the south. On the other end, nothing has been erected to distinguish property. The beit to the north has fragrant jasmine bushes creating a makeshift border. The neighbor's children are constructing something with branches and rocks and glance over at us when we appear then ignore us for the rest of the time my father attempts to make amends.

"Allah forgive an unkind word against the deceased," he begins. His eyebrows are unwieldy and sparse. The sun here has bronzed his hands and face with a healthy hue in spite of his age. The wrinkles around his eyes are joyful ones, and I feel my stomach tightening with anger as I recall my mother's deeply grooved face, the lines in her forehead that tightened when she spoke long-distance to her brother.

"I loved your mother for many years," he tells me. "I don't know what happened between us, but I couldn't live with her anymore. A mother and a wife are two separate women."

"Very wise words," I say, snapping a leaf off the fig tree.

"Why do you have to be difficult, ya Madeeha? Why can't we begin here and let the past go?"

"Because the past always invades the present, Baba!" It's the first time I call him this in over ten years and I begin to cry.

He sits down on one of the stools and folds his hands in his lap. He looks very old. I sit, too, wiping my eyes and nose with the back of my hand, and we both watch the children next door. An impressively leafy fortress slowly emerges, obscuring their lower bodies as they kneel in the red dirt.

"Where's your hawiya?" One child demands, pretending to be an Israeli soldier at a checkpoint. "Hand over your identification card! Now!"

My father reaches over and lightly touches my fingers. "Inshallah you can forgive me, Madeeha. You're my only daughter. We're all we have now."

I continue to observe the children who fight over how high they want to build. I am amazed at how quickly a wall has been erected.

* * *

Over half a century ago, my father first saw my mother at the souq, boldly sidling up to her and asking for her name.

Can you believe his nerve! my mother had exclaimed when she told me this story. I was ten years old, rummaging through her old photo albums for a school project on family trees and had come across a picture of her standing in front of a small stone house, holding an orange. Palm trees shaded one part of her face like a partially dropped veil.

She took the photograph from my hand. *Look at me back then! How naïve! I should have realized your father was trouble.*

That day at the souq, he was utterly rebuked in front of his friends when my mother had pretended to spit on the ground near his feet—dramatic enough to arouse the attention of customers and vendors nearby. An old man raised his cane, ready to strike at my father in defense of a young, single woman. She finally interceded on my father's behalf, placating the old hajj. She touched the old man's shoulder and he lowered his cane.

I was afraid some of the other men would pummel your father! she told me. I had not thought this part was funny, but my mother giggled like a teenager, pulled back to that carefree time when she had believed in romantic destiny, yet still played the part of a proper arabiya with a reputation to protect.

So why did you marry Baba? I asked.

Why wouldn't I? she retorted. *He was handsome, making good money abroad. He was my ticket to the United States.*

But you loved him, right? I had been too young to appreciate that unhappy endings were common endings. At the time, I felt a pang of resentment towards my mother. My father had seemed doting and generous. He never laid a finger on me, leaving the harshest punishments to my mother.

Not all at once, my mother informed me, still gazing at her photograph. *But, oh, the time we had courting!*

After that fateful meeting at the souq, my father hailed a cab for my mother and asked for her address to give to the driver.

You think I'm a fool? my mother had demanded, still playing coy. *I'll tell the driver as soon as he drives away from you.*

You're a hard one, Miss, my father laughed. *But, I'll find you again. You don't let a fine jewel slip into the sand.*

In spite of herself, she had blushed. My father carefully closed the passenger door and tapped the roof of the cab. My mother, sweetly agitated by the encounter, fumbled her address to the driver. I imagined the cab driver watching her in his rearview mirror as she couldn't help smiling the whole way home.

* * *

Khalo Rizq invites my father and his wife to lunch the next day. Over Nadira's delicious mlookhiya, my uncle and father make small talk about the sulta—the Palestinian Authority—and their latest indiscretions as Nadira and I gather spoonfuls of the dark, leafy stew and pour it over our individual plates of rice. I notice we aren't eating from a large family platter—all of us at once dipping our spoons or forks into whatever heaping meal my uncle's wife had prepared. It is a deliberate gesture by Nadira, to serve my father with a solitary plate.

After clearing the table at the end of the meal, I'm cornered by my uncle in the tiny kitchen.

"He's trying at least," Khalo Rizq tells me in a low voice.

The same children are playing in the backyard, laughing and shrieking as they chase each other. I silently arrange tiny demitasse cups and saucers on a silver tray while Nadira stands over the stove, minding the thick coffee bubbling in a small brass pot. Cardamom infuses the air in this small space. Every few seconds, my uncle's wife pulls the pot by its long handle away from the flame and carefully returns it until it's frothy. She listens as my uncle tries to persuade me, her mouth turned down at the corners in disapproval. And though I know nothing of their relationship, I sense how much my mother meant to Nadira, and like me, she feels it's a betrayal if I make amends. I hardly know Nadira, but my stomach flutters with the prospect of missing her when I leave in eleven more days.

After each cup has been poured full of rich qahwa, I lift the tray and turn to my uncle.

"Alright," I tell him, avoiding Nadira's eyes. "I'll spend some time with him."

After coffee, I agree to have my father escort me through Ramallah so I can shop for souvenirs. He drives an old 1990 BMW and holds open the passenger door for me. Taxicabs speed along Al Sharafa Street and I discover there are more of them than regular cars on the road.

My father turns on the ignition and swiftly merges into traffic to a cacophony of honks. From a dusty cassette player, Abdel Halim Hafez, a famous Egyptian singer, croons a mellifluous ballad about harmless flirtation.

It is in the public market that I'm aware of my bare head. Men slow down to gawk as I walk past, some attempt to rub up against me, grazing my arm. My father grits his teeth and moves ahead of me like a football offensive lineman. I notice only a few of the women are without hijab, but they are wearing tiny crucifixes around their necks and long-sleeved blouses.

"You should be covering your head," he grumbles. "You're lucky this isn't Gaza."

Children with dirty faces and missing teeth swarm us when we get to the fruit market.

"Miska, miska!" they cry out in unison. "Three packs of gum for three shekels!"

My father swats at them like flies. "Leave us alone, ya loolad! We don't want any!"

I stop and fish into my oversized leather purse and pull out my wallet. I haven't changed my American dollars, yet. I extract two five-dollar bills.

"What are you doing?" My father gasps. "Don't waste your money!"

It feels delicious to openly defy my father. I hand my bills over to two of the older boys with buzz cuts and dirty fingernails. "Keep your gum," I tell them.

A little boy wraps his arm around my waist and squeezes me. "Shookrun ikteer, Miss!"

"You're welcome," I say.

My father stomps ahead of me. I smile impishly behind my shades.

The streets of the hisbah are strewn with fugitive plastic bags and rotten fruit smashed beyond recognition near the curbs. The vendors' stalls are a kaleidoscope of auburgine, yellow, green, and red vegetables. My father haggles with a vendor for a dozen guava fruit.

"Try this jowafa," he tells me. He wipes the fruit on his shirt and hands it to me.

I bite into the soft yellow flesh and hundreds of tiny edible seeds surprise me. It's deliciously sweet and tangy. "It's good," I concede.

My father smiles, glad we've agreed on something.

Merchants smoke and sip tea outside their storefronts. There are competing thoub tailors, vetting their beautifully sewn dresses with cross-stitched flowers and birds in flight.

The only time my mother ever wore a thoub was the night before her wedding. She wore a red-velvet one with a wide band tied around her waist and a coin-lined headdress. In one photograph, she holds her hands up to the camera, the homemade henna her mother-in-law—my grandmother—spread in her palms. My father wore a keffiyah and abaya and the two of them looked like a traditional fellahi couple on display in a museum.

I wouldn't be caught dead in one of those again, she always said when we leafed through old albums with sticky pages. *Your father's side always resented that I was a mediniyah.*

She waved that city-dweller mentality in my father's face like the imperial staff of a contemptuous queen. My father had never minded so long as she was a good wife, but I'll never know about that. He was right: a wife and mother are two separate women and she was a good mother. The moments in between eluded me as do with most children who expect their parents to be together no matter how much it pained them.

I purchase a scarf the color of a garnet and tie it around my head before we leave the store. My father smiles with approval.

On our way back to El Bireh, my father suggests I visit Dar el Neesat, a charitable organization run exclusively by women.

"They make special clothes and crafts and sell them. The proceeds go to the needy families in the camps," he says. "To the widows of martyrs. I bet you'll find some nice things to take back home. Basima volunteers there, too."

"I'm tired," I tell him. I want to go back to Khalo Rizq's flat. I calculate the time it must be in Chicago and wonder what Ata is doing. Has he done his own laundry yet or accumulated enough plates and coffee mugs for a cycle in the dishwasher? I miss him terribly. If he were here, he would be lightly squeezing my thigh or pressing his fingers into my palm, reminding me to keep things on an even keel with my father.

"Tired from a little shopping?" my father says. He gives me a sidelong glance as he beeps at a slower moving car he's been trying to pass up. "Shoo mallak, ya zalama? Can't you drive, man?" he shouts out the window.

"We'll just say a quick hello," he says, jerking around the other car as soon as he gets a chance. He cheerfully waves in the rear view mirror to a succession of angry honks.

* * *

Inside Dar el Neesat is a small museum devoted to the history of El Bireh as one of the largest municipalities in the West Bank. There are pre-1948 black and white prints of the landscape from Jabil al-Taweel to Nablus Road, low mountains speckled with thorn bushes and valleys with herds of goat. My father's clan, Qorr'aan, along with Abed and Hamayal clans, is portrayed in patriarchal poses with men in checkered keffiyahs standing behind their seated women with children in their laps. They all stare at the camera lens and do not smile.

The director greets us in one of the galleries. "Mashallah, this is your daughter?" she exclaims, grabbing my hands. "She looks just like her mother, God rest her soul! What is your name, habibti"?

"Madeeha."

"Like that old Egyptian actress?" She throws her head back and laughs, utterly bemused by this. She's the first middle-aged woman I've seen here not wearing hijab. In fact, she looks like a banker in her green tailored dress with gold buttons running all the way down to the hem just below her knees. Her hair is stylishly coiffed and her face is lightly made up.

"Come this way," she instructs us, still holding one of my hands. "Let me show you our operation."

We walk down a narrow corridor and into a large workspace. Twenty sewing machines are stationed in neat rows, women hunched over them as they move fabric through the biting needles. Spools of thread whirl. A few of the women glance up at us when the director waves a hand over them, saying proudly, "Like busy bees these women are, mashallah!"

We walk a few paces down one row and a woman turns her face up to look at me. Her right eye is closed, the lid sealed shut, and I could see the outline of her eyeball, slightly bobbing beneath the lid as though it were a fetus rippling against its mother's taut skin. I quickly look away.

Then I notice other workers with defects. Some are prominent like a woman who's missing her lower arm, yet can still skillfully handle the sewing machine with the single hand of her good arm. Others are less discernible like a woman seated a few stations behind her. This one's measuring fabric and I discover small stumps where two fingers should be. The worst is one who appears younger than me holding up a finished amethyst-colored abaya. Scar tissue stretches diagonally from her right temple beneath her hijab, to her opposite ear as though she had been unable to turn away in time to avoid a splash of burning chemicals. The rest of her skin is olive and clear.

"Were they all injured in the war?" I quietly ask.

"What war?" my father scoffs. "It's an invasion."

"How's Basima?" the director asks my father. "She's one of our best volunteers." She directs this comment to me and I pretend not to hear. The whirring of spools of thread and drilling of needles rise to a din. I glance back at the young woman with the sealed eyelid. Her shoulders are curved as she moves fabric through the machine.

"You rescued her, may Allah bestow blessings upon you," the director says. "What's a young widow to do in these terrible times?" To me, "When you're a woman you naturally sacrifice everything."

"She's a widow?" I turn to my father. "You didn't tell me that."

"And with two young boys," the director adds, nodding. I watch my father's face harden and his eyes narrow, but she doesn't seem to notice and prattles on. "If it weren't for your father, she'd be just another widow of this godforsaken occupation."

"Where are the children?" I ask. "Do they live with you?" For a moment, I feel something close to joy, the sensation that perhaps something good is near. My father has been given this chance to redeem himself, to make up for his absence from my life by being present for two young boys—half-orphans, like me. A rush of magnanimity courses through my chest.

"That's not how things are done here, Madeeha," my father says in English. "Basima can see them as much as she wants and I buy them whatever they need."

The blood pools hot in my cheeks. My scalp tingles and itches.

The director looks between my father and me, sensing a tension that seems to surprise her. Khair inshallah! She grabs my arm. "What's wrong, habibti?"

I pull off the hijab from the crown of my head, but the knot at the base of my throat has become as tight as a noose. I fumble to loosen it, almost clawing at it, to be free of the flimsy fabric whose purchase had satisfied my father at the souk.

"How could you leave those kids behind? How could you do something like that again?" My body trembles as I take a step closer to my father, both of my hands clutching the headscarf. I cling to it for balance, composure, afraid if I let it drop to the floor, I might strike my father. In front of us, rows of women busily sew, oblivious to another family scandal my father has created.

"Madeeha," my father begins, but my voice lunges.

"No!"

Several women stop sewing and soon the workspace is like a gigantic machine grinding to a halt as they turn watch us. "You've kept her from her children," I spit at him. "That's terrible. You're a terrible man, Baba."

* * *

Amti Nabeeha is my father's paternal aunt, a woman who's never been married—a fact I found incredible when I first met her the day most of the family came to greet me. My father asked if I'd like him to take me to her beit for a customary visit of an elderly relative, but I have refused to go any place with him since I'd found out about Basima's children. Not even Khalo Rizq can convince me to be anywhere near him. I decide to walk to Amti Nabeeha's house, which is only a half-mile from Khalo Rizq's beit.

Nadira draws me an easy map and I trek along El Sharafa Street until I come to a small store that sells used bicycles. I head east toward Jabal El Taweel, a tall mountain separating the village from a compound of Israeli settlers on the other side. In the distance, I see Al Uma'ari refugee camp densely packed with cinderblock houses. A line of smoke swirls into the sky from a corner of the camp—the burning of garbage when the municipality neglects to come and gather it.

It seems natural to wave to young and old women sitting on their barranda, shelling watermelon seeds or drinking tea. They wave back and some call to me, "Itfadallee! Please join us!" I'm not unfamiliar with such easy hospitality from Arabs—its boundless volume at every turn overwhelms me.

When I enter Amti Nabeeha's beit, my nostrils are assaulted by the odor of lamb which my mother could never make me eat no matter how much coaxing she did when I was a kid. There's a large steel pot over a low flame on the stove in the kitchen, but Amti Nabeeha is not inside. I carefully remove the lid and lamb shanks are boiling inside. A white, foamy substance floats like flotsam on the surface. I used to watch my mother standing by the stove with her large wooden spoon, ready to scrape the froth away from the meat.

"A closed lid keeps the juices sealed inside the meat," my mother had told me as I stood next to her, my head barely reaching her shoulder at the time. "What escapes must be removed so the water can continue to boil."

Instinctively, I scrape away the froth from the lamb shanks the way my mother showed me without removing the bulk of the water. Then I go search for Amti Nabeeha.

I walk around her beit and find her bent over at the waist, vigorously yanking weeds from a large patch of mint stalks. Her behind is wide and round like a barrel, concealing her torso. I'm impressed with such nimbleness in a ninety-year-old body.

"Salam alaykum," I say, not too loudly to keep from startling the old woman.

She slowly rises up and turns a step a time to face me. "Ahlan, ahlan," she greets me. Most of her teeth are missing save her incisors and lower molars. "It's about time you paid me a visit. I was thinking you were putting on airs like your mother did—Allah rest her soul. Even so, I loved her most of all the wives of my sons and nephews."

This old woman raised my father after his mother—my grandmother Suhair—died when he was ten years old. I didn't get a chance to meet my grandfather who passed away only a month after my father settled back in El Bireh. He'd at least gotten to attend his father's funeral.

I guide Amti Nabeeha by her elbow to a fig tree and hold her steady as she lowers herself onto a roped stool. I sit beside her, at her feet, on a long faded mat. She offers me loquats from a small bowl. The yellow fruit is ripe and juicy and I easily consume two clusters, spitting the seeds over my shoulder and they disappear into the rocky earth that surrounds us.

"It's good, mish ah?" Amti Nabeeha plucks a few leaves off of another cluster in the bowl and hands them to me. "You travelled here just in time to eat some. This is the last eskadinyah of the season."

"How are you, Amti?" I ask the old woman. Thin gray hairs peek out of a wine-red scarf, tied behind her head so the sagging flesh of her neck is exposed. Along the bridge of her nose is a burst of freckles. Her eyebrows are sparse and a few tiny white whiskers jut out of her small chin.

"Elhamdulillah," she tells me. "No better, no worse."

"Shall I turn off the stove?" I wonder how soon before the water is completely absorbed in the pot.

"No, no. The shanks still have a good hour yet before they're cooked."

She's laid out a tattered, but clean towel with mlookhiya stems and motions for me to pick one up. She gathers several stems in her lap and demonstrates how to snip each leaf from the stem and toss it onto a large platter near her feet.

"Like this," she instructs me. She is swift and steady, her liver-spotted hand discarding one naked stem after another to the ground. "So how are you enjoying your visit so far? Inshallah, it's been good.

"Elhamdulillah, fine. Exhausting, too," I say. "I'm trying to see everyone before I leave in a week."

"So soon, ya binit?!" Amti Nabeeha exclaims. She's plucked nearly a dozen stems to my five. I try to pick up the pace.

"I have to get back to my job, Amti," I tell her. "A person has only so much time before they're replaced."

"How true," she says. "You're lucky to have choices. To be able to see the sights of this bilad, eat some eskadinyah, visit folks you'll probably never lay eyes on again. Then you'll get on a plane back to your easy life."

I shrug. Unlike morning and evening of each day, afternoons here seem to stretch forever. I haven't seen many clouds, only sun, and I consider how much I would miss the seasons of Illinois, the cumulus clouds and the first crispy day of October and the day grass returns—first wispy before becoming full blades.

The call for prayer will sound soon. And I know that I will greatly miss this part of my trip. I've come to look forward to this rich and sonorous disruption. Though nothing really changes, it somehow feels like time stops for a moment. "We all have to go back to our lives at some point, I suppose."

"Yes. I guess you're right," Amti Nabeeha says. "Some of us try a new direction."

I remain silent. I can see where this is going, but I don't want to be disrespectful. I just nod my head.

"How are you getting along with your father's wife? What's her name? Buthayna?"

"Basima," I say.

"She laughs like an idiot sometimes, but there's no harm in that," Amti Nabeeha says.

Before I can stop myself, I blurt out, "How could she give up her kids? How could my father let her?" I can't look at Amti's face, but I sense she's stopped plucking the mlookhiya leaves. She waves a stem under my nose and I look up.

"What do you know about life here?" she demands. "She couldn't retrieve her husband's body for days, waiting for a damned permit just to cross into Tel Aviv." Amti Nabeeha's words whistle through her remaining teeth.

"I don't know anything about her," I say defiantly, ignoring these awful details. "Why should I care? He left my mother and me then married a woman half his age. And she abandoned her own children to be with that selfish jerk!" The last part I say in English and the old woman can only guess its import.

"I cannot speak for your father, child," she says. "But, you think Basima had a choice? Is that what you think?" She chuckles and shakes her head. "Ya rabbi, I envy your ignorance."

"Tell me, then, how could she have not had a choice!"

Amti Nabeeha drops the leafy stems back onto the clean towel and gathers a silver container of snuff. She methodically rolls a cigarette as she speaks. "I'll tell you, ya binit. Patience." She lights up and deeply inhales, letting the smoke stream out of her nose. She cups her elbow in one hand while taking drags from her thin and moist cigarette.

"She was pregnant with her youngest boy, close to birth. It's a wonder the shock didn't induce labor or kill that child inside her." Amti Nabeeha coughs and spits phlegm into an empty canister that has a picture of a leaping ghazal on it. I have seen it many times before in my mother's kitchen. It contained a special brand of shortening that she always requested when family and friends visited overseas. She never asked for anything else—just that samna. She said it was the most important ingredient in the date-filled ka'ak cookies she made every eid.

Amti Nabeeha continues. "Her husband—may he rest in peace—had been returning with a group of men outside Tel Aviv very late at night. They had just finished quarry work—no doubt the stones for a new settlement. Allah sting their hearts with bitterness, those yahood! He had been gone for more than a month. I imagine his firstborn had already been taking his first steps—maybe walking steady in his father's absence."

"From what the gossips have told me, Basima was beside herself with joy and excitement. She had been planning a small azzouma for his return and she and the neeswan in her family spent three days baking dozens of ikras sabanagh."

The old woman shifts on her stool, and ashes fall from her cigarette. "I, unluckily, cannot eat those spinach pies—I get horrible heartburn. When I was girl I could eat them morning, noon, and night."

The muezzin begins his call for the early evening prayer. The sun sinks lower but still blindingly shines over the village. A bird flits between the fig and loquat tree.

"My mother baked ikras at least once a month and froze batches of them so I could eat them whenever I wanted," I tell the old woman. The sound of my voice surprises me like someone creeping up behind me, scaring me for a moment until I recognize who it is.

Amti Nabeeha gives me a toothless grin and pats my cheek. Her fingers stink of tobacco and earth. "Who doesn't love ikras? But, Basima never had a chance to enjoy serving them. She had been planning a feast then found herself preparing a funeral." She pauses and presses her thin lips to her cigarette.

"All of the men in that truck had valid I.D.s—they'd been going in and out of Israel for years to work. It was their fate, I suppose. You can't predict a person's bakht. One minute you're living in relative peace, the next you're gunned down because you defy an order to get out of a truck." Amti Nabeeha takes one more drag then moistens her fingertips and puts out her cigarette. "Of course, that's the official version, you understand." She pinches the burnt tip and places it inside her snuff case.

I nod mutely. I try not to imagine each man in the cramped truck, lurching from machine gun bullets, their arms flopping for a few seconds before their chests fold over their knees. Perhaps their bodies leaned on one another, each man's head resting on the shoulder of another as they drew their final breaths.

When Amti Nabeeha heaves herself up, her bones creak and I quickly stand to help her.

"May Allah bestow upon us only that which we can endure," Amti Nabeeha sighs, grabbing my forearm so I can lead her inside. "I'd better pray before I lose my wudu. At this age, it gets harder to wash your feet."

* * *

After practiced coaxing from Khalo Rizq, I find myself seated between my father and a woman who's sharing our taxicab to the Dead Sea. She smells of lemons and zaatar—crushed thyme. We wait ten minutes until Mahmoud Abbas's caravan passes. The president is driven in a sleek black BMW with gilded Palestinian flags jutting above the hood and rear tires. A few stopped cars jubilantly honk, but my father unabashedly curses the sulta inside our cab.

"He's no better than a collaborator," he tells the driver who appears to agree, but remains silent. "What's he done except split our country into two? One even more squalid than before the Israelis had control over it."

The woman seated on my left remains silent except when she sucks on her teeth as though to punctuate my father's admonitions of the leadership. She appears to be in her forties and a row of golden bangles occasional jingle when she raises her arm to clutch the handrail over the window. On Nablus Road, we pass sprawling villas with bougainvillea crawling up stone hedges. We pass refugee camps with asymmetrical houses covered in corrugated tin.

Some children ride their rusty bicycles around pools of standing water while others chase them on foot.

I can feel my father's gaze as I peer out the window. That morning, Basima sent along small glass jars for collecting mud from the Dead Sea and now they roll inside a plastic bag on the floor of the cab and clink together with each bump of the road. Souvenirs for a few nurses at the hospital and my closest girlfriends, all of whom I'll be seeing in a few more days when I return to the States. Basima is unable to accompany us without a proper hawiya and I learn she had never seen the Dead Sea and has traveled only once to Jerusalem for eid prayers when she was a teenager—and once to Tel Aviv to collect her first husband's body. Um Kalthum sings low on the driver's cassette player and I recognize the ballad as one my mother hummed while she cooked.

After an hour, we arrive in Jericho in a small area of store fronts and fruit vendors where the woman passenger leaves our company. A young man standing outside a white hatchback, splotchy with rust, waves at her and she scurries over to him with some packages the driver had stored in the cab's trunk. She gives him a hearty kiss on each cheek before relinquishing the packages to him.

The driver recommends a small café a few yards along the dusty road and my father and I walk without speaking, the space between us wide enough for another person to comfortably occupy. The café sign reads "Ya Halla" and is painted in black letters at a slant above the wide-open doors. In front of the café a few wooden round tables with chairs are empty except for an old man smoking a hookah. He nods at us when my father greets him.

I order a fruit cocktail, which I see the owner scoop out of a can in the back kitchen, though the menu says it's fresh. The owner is also the server and he brings it over with a bottle of Coca Cola for my father. They chat for a bit as I take small spoonfuls of the warm fruit cocktail and gaze into the hazy distance. Palm trees line the single road and idle men sit on straw mats beneath their shade. When the café owner returns to the kitchen I wait for my father to tell me about the honeymoon he and my mother had taken to this town and to offer a quick stop at the small house where they had stayed, but he doesn't. And, I don't ask.

The driver beeps his horn to signal it's time to go. We drive along the wadi of low-slung mountains where Bedouin tents flap in the warm wind. Brown and white sheep hides hang on wooden racks and a row of enormous tin pans glint in the sunlight. Cheese-cloths suspended near the opening of the tents are heavy with yogurt, dripping their excess moisture into pots positioned beneath them. Then the road narrows and we move between steep, rocky walls until the sea opens before us.

The Dead Sea is a shimmering expanse of turquoise. I leave the cab and walk towards the beach, removing my sandals when the pavement becomes sand. I stare, amazed, as the sea is much bluer than I had imagined or how photographs had depicted. My father brings out a picnic of hummus sandwiches and open-face ground beef ishfeeha that Basima had wrapped in foil and a clean dishtowel. The driver removes his shoes and socks, rolls up his khaki pants, and wades near the shore. He appears contentedly detached from the rest of us.

The din of laughter and chatter from tourists floating on their backs rises and falls as I cautiously approach the sea, their joy is suspicious to me. I worry I'll be temporarily blinded by the salt and I'll need help returning to shore. I refuse to be vulnerable. Slowly, the distance between me and the sea recedes and it begins licking my toes. I venture a few more feet until my calves are completely submerged in the warm water.

My father follows closely behind me and waits until I stop pushing forward. When I choose a wading spot, he approaches me like a tentative stranger about to ask for directions.

"Your mother and I honeymooned in Jericho, where we stopped earlier. Did you know that?"

"She had mentioned it before," I say, remembering the sepia-colored photograph of my mother holding an orange.

I watch young blonde children scooping mud into the small hands and smearing it on each other's faces and laughing. Their bikini-clad mother speaks to them in a European dialect I can't discern. I remember the glass jars on the floor of the cab and imagine Basima here for the first time bending over to touch the water with her fingertips, the hem of her dishdasha grazing its surface and soaking it into blackness. I imagine her sons, one bolting into the sea, kicking up water in his wake while the other boy chases him with hands in front of his face, shielding his eyes against the salty wetness. I'm not certain about many things, but I know deep in my bones that Basima and her sons will never experience the sea. It is a gaping hole in their falasteeniya existence that they'll fill with other stuff: grief for a martyred husband, hope in a second marriage, painful love for children, boundless adoration of grandchildren, and death.

"We were at the souq and she stopped by a peddler with a broken down cart. He had a block of concrete holding up one end so all his junk wouldn't fall over," my father recalls. "Your mother rummaged through the cheap bangles and shawls until she found a charm—*el ayn*, warder of the evil eye. She said I needed to buy it immediately." My father chuckles. "'*To protect our love from envious eyes,*' your mother said. I never believed in that stuff, but she insisted." He turns to me. "Did she ever show it to you?"

"No," I say flatly and it's a lie. A week after she died, I came across a red velvet box on the top shelf of her closet. The chain is thinly braided silver and an oval-shaped eye hangs from it. I had tried it on, fingering it as I sat on my mother's empty bed. But, I don't tell my father this—not yet.

My father shifts his body and I sense his disappointment. "I wish things could be different for you and me, Madeeha," he says, his gaze straight ahead as we wade side by side. This has become our natural stance—to look in the same direction, yet never at each other. His words muffle every sound around me: a toddler crying in its father's arms, children tagging each other. It's not an apology, an admission of wrong-doing, because it's become irrelevant now, today, in this moment. It's more or less a declaration of the future, of moving forward. Like Basima did, and the disfigured widows of Dar el Neesat, continually spooling thread and pedaling at their machines.

He touches my shoulder and it's as gentle as a butterfly alighting on a flower then is gone. He moves away from me as though he has come dangerously close, and begins a slow trek back to the shore.

Tears sting my eyes and the glaring sun creates a haze over the sea. The mountains of Jordan appear like a dream in the distance. I dig my toes deep into the silky silt. The absence of green is so powerful that it feels like a presence here. I think of the craters that were found by the deep-sea divers and consider how life still springs from unlikely places.

Acknowledgments

These stories have been lovingly cradled and nurtured by many individuals, beginning with my dearest friend, Anita Dellaria, my very first fan. She heard my voice and saw me through crises of stagnation and insecurity. Her critical eye and a genuine quest for hope and beauty in stories continuously elevate my writing. I hope to acquire her grace and kindness that a true artist possesses.

And a most sincere, though quite inadequate thanks to the following: my mentor and MFA advisor Patricia McNair, whose guidance at Columbia College Chicago ushered these stories to fruition; the Fiction Writing Department of Columbia College Chicago and my talented peers who challenged me; Megan Stielstra, who emulates the power and compassion of strong female writers who pave the way; my devoted colleagues at Homewood-Flossmoor High School, who've supported this wonderful second life of mine; the brilliant and tireless editors of valuable literary magazines and journals whose faith and dedication coaxed these stories to their fullest potential; Radius of Arab American Writers, who provided me with a community; and the Willow Books family and Aquarius Press, including Heather Buchanan and Randall Horton, who've provided a space for diverse voices.

Finally, heartfelt gratitude to my lovely and patient daughters, Sabah and Sabrine, and my husband Khalid; to my deceased father, Ismail Mustafa; to my mother, Mariam Qafisheh; to my sisters and brothers Hala, Abeer, Linda, Feras and Mori; and to other generous relatives and dear friends who were in the audience when I shared these stories with the world. Thanks for listening.

"New and Gently Used Hijab" appeared in *Room* (2016) and was a 2016 Pushcart nominee; "Failed Treaties" appeared in *The Bellevue Literary Review* (2015) and was named a Distinguished Story by *Best American Short Stories* (2016); "Code of the West" appeared in *American Fiction* (2015) by New Rivers Press and was an American Fiction Prize Finalist; "Wingspan" appeared in *Hair Trigger* (2015) and was the recipient of the David Friedman Award for Best Fiction; "The Great Chicago Fire" appeared in *Story Magazine* (2015); "Shisha Love" appeared in *Word Riot* (2012), won the Guild Literary Complex Prize for Prose, and was a 2013 Pushcart nominee; "Perfect Genes" and "Widow" appeared in *Hair Trigger* (respectively 2013, 2014).

About the Author

Sahar Mustafah is the daughter of Palestinian immigrants, a richly complicated inheritance she explores in her fiction.